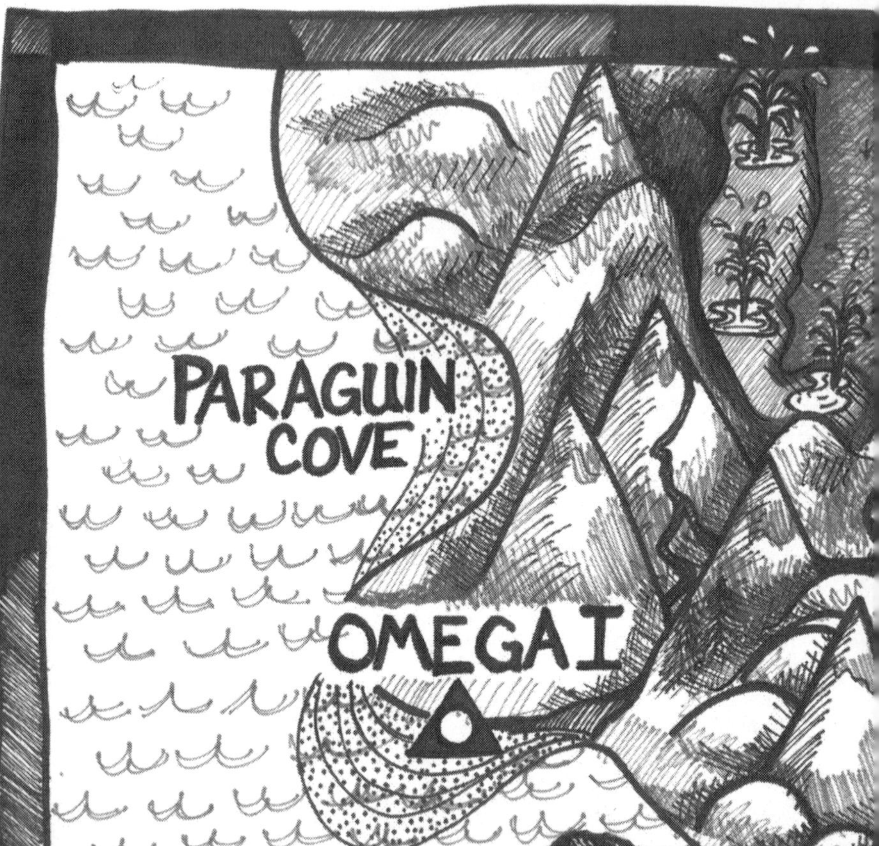
PARAGUIN COVE
OMEGA I

OMEGA II

N ↑

Mission to
Green Tara

a Bosque Family Adventure

By

K. H. Brower

Addie & Drinan,
Thank you for doing all you can to protect the living waters of our amazing planet.
K.H.B.

This book is a work of fiction. Names, characters, places, and incidents are a product of the author's imagination or are used fictitiously. Any resemblance to actual events, locales, or persons, living or dead, is coincidental.

Copyright © 2013 by K.H. Brower

All rights reserved. In accordance with the U.S. Copyright Act of 1976, the scanning, uploading, and electronic sharing of any part of this book without permission of the publisher constitute unlawful piracy and theft of the author's intellectual property. If you would like to use material from the book (other than for review purposes), prior written permission must be obtained by contacting the publisher. Thank you for your support of the author's rights.

Scramjet Books
3689 S. Sowder Square
Bloomington, Indiana 47401

First Edition 2013

ISBN 978-0-9887911-1-4

⊕

Dedication

I dedicate *Mission to Green Tara* to Nancy Sullivan, my second mom and the woman who first taught me that protecting our natural environment is a noble calling.

Scientific Inspiration

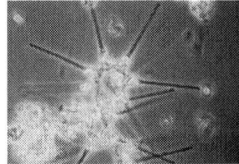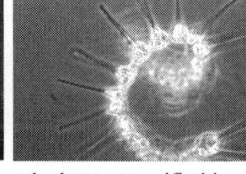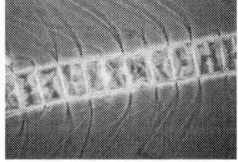

Three varieties of phytoplankton: magnified images courtesy of NOAA

Phytoplankton are single-celled plants that live in the upper, sunlit layer of our oceans. These diverse and plentiful plants generate 70-90% of the oxygen for our planet in a process called photosynthesis.

Water ecosystems depend on phytoplankton as a source of food. In the intricate web of life all oxygen-breathing creatures on Earth, even those that live on land or in the air, also depend on these microscopic life forms.

⊕

⊕

Unauthorized Test Flight

I never thought I'd get caught.

Getting past security was the tricky part, and I made it through all the check points without a second glance from the crew. I used a couple of simple strategies, like acting the part of *pilot-on-a-mission*, and it was ridiculously easy to get off deck.

My purpose? I could say I was practicing to save a planet. Or, I could say I had a terrible fight with my dad, and that I reacted impulsively, defying authority in the biggest way possible. But either excuse would be a lie. I never lie. I do admit to breaking rules when they're irrational—and onboard ship there are an infinite number of those.

Here's the truth: I wanted to be outside of all the suffocating rules, soaring.

I took a deep, satisfying breath. My flight plan was flawless.

Everything felt so spacious. Even though I knew the oxygen capacity of my tiny scramjet was minuscule compared to the mammoth mother ship, I breathed more deeply when I was on my own. And when my lungs expanded I felt larger, more grown up.

This was what it was like to fly solo.

I felt peaceful.

A chime sounded, and the navigation display on the console read: *Flight Plan Midpoint*, and, flashing in orange, *Return to Ship*.

I wasn't ready to go back. Not even close. My Blast flew like a dream. The simulator was a cramped closet compared to this. Of course, I knew the risk of ignoring the navigation alert, but I needed to fly! I spun away, practicing sharp maneuvers in my smooth little ride.

A yellow bar on the console rolled open and more words lit up: *Engaging Auto-Pilot*.

Zap. I flipped the bar over. "Cancel the auto. I'm the pilot." Under my control, the Blast spun starboard, and the view from my seat downgraded from perfect starscape to the potbellied eyesore, my home. Then, the mother ship belched.

Of course I couldn't hear a belch. I couldn't hear any sounds from the ship because sound doesn't travel in deep space. But that's how it looked—belchy. The big, old ship belched aft gasses, again, and then ... ewww. Who needs to see a ship spewing refuse? "From out here home looks ..." I searched for a good way to describe it. If I'd had deep feelings for it, I might have said the colonial cruise ship looked sad.

"...Ill-fitting?" Dot suggested from her position, spread out on the console just inside the window.

Dot had a way with words, but the dumping action called for rude and crude. "I was thinking it looks like a bucket o' farts." I laughed so hard it came out like a snort.

"Virginia, that is not a very civilized way to describe our home." Dot used her most prim tutor voice. It wasn't a reprimand, though. I've had Dot, my personal information, retrieval, and storage device, my whole life, and I knew she was teasing me. I could tell by the smile lines crinkling at the outside corners of her eyes.

The orange panel on the navigation display flashed again. Dot said, "If you stay outside your allotted flight time, without a doubt, you will trigger an investigation."

I didn't push the limits anymore. I set course for our return to ship.

When I made it back to K-Deck, I pulled my Blast in between two larger scramjets to remain inconspicuous and cut my hover engine. Touch down. I picked Dot up and wrapped her around my forearm in transport mode. "We made it, Dot. See. No worries."

She looked up at me and said, "I take it you think your unauthorized test flight has been worth the risk?"

"Is a blue star hot?"

"Let me check my database." She flicked her eyes left, up, right ... a quicksilver roll of the eyes.

I pressed her face flap closed to avoid her critical stare, popped open the back hatch, and slipped out of my Blast. The oxygen generator rumbled, something I felt more than heard, and I sucked in the stale air.

Even though I was back in time, something about my flight must have set off an alert, because two men in gray jumpsuits met me on the ramp—sentries. And the sentries were holding weapons.

I peeled back Dot's face flap and whispered, "Why didn't you warn me?"

She just gave me that I-told-you-so look, and her screen went blank.

Great. Nothing like being abandoned and left in the custody of a couple of hyper-vigilant sentries who, as it turned out, were there to escort me to lockdown. They had a summons for me. Me! I never, ever expected to be taken to lockdown. That's where they put frightening, high-security-risk rebels. Not a teenage girl.

Now I was going to have to explain to my dad how I'd gotten off deck without a license.

⊕

Lockdown

Somewhere near the lockdown entrance, the sentries shoved me into a scanning chamber and then left me alone for an excessive amount of time. Clearly, they weren't in any hurry—I'm guessing they decided to take a bio-break—and I felt my adrenaline drop. I slid to the bare floor and buried my face into Dot's plush side.

After a brief soft and fuzzy moment, I thought about how I'd gotten in this ugly spot. "Dot."

Her quicksilver eyes blinked open. "Yes?"

"I hate you. You're supposed to protect me." I'm not proud of it, but I'm sure I was whining like a little girl.

Dot said, "You knew you were breaking protocol."

"But I stayed within my flight plan limits." I was hurt and frustrated. But I wasn't really angry with her, and I didn't want to argue. She was right. I knew I'd been breaking the rules. My mouth was so dry, it hurt to swallow. I needed to remember what was so wonderful about taking my Blast for a test ride, because I was definitely paying a steep price. I managed a few words. "Let's review the flight footage." I whispered, "Please."

Without hesitation, Dot opened a motion picture recording of the star view from my pilot's seat, and mentally, if not physically, I was back in the vast, raw beauty of deep space. Blazing bolides, I'd actually done it!

Suddenly, the chamber door cracked wide open, bringing me back to the less-than-perfect situation.

The sentries motioned for me to follow, then pushed me through an inky black corridor that dropped us into lockdown.

The walls and ceiling had a slick sheen. So did the floor. The sentries' boot steps bounced off the dark, cold surfaces, and the hollow sound made my stomach lurch.

The sentries led me past an interrogation bench where a young man in an olive green uniform sat hunched over. He looked vaguely familiar, and when he glanced up, I remembered him. It was the same crewman who'd given me clearance to take off from the flight deck a few hours earlier. He winced and looked back down at the floor. He was wearing light bands on his arms, and two rows were lit up. That meant he was getting punished. I recognized the device and knew basically how it was used, but it was tough to see on a real person, up close and personal.

An interrogator growled at him, "Explain." An official SensEye floating in the center of the room focused on him, too.

A bead of sweat dropped from his forehead onto his badge. I could see his name—Ray. He said, "I'm not sure why the craft didn't raise an alert. But it's a convertible scramjet, flight worthy in zero-to-full atmosphere, so it's been modified. Maybe when it was re-engineered the security sensors were disabled."

I thought Ray made an excellent analysis of the situation. I know my dad made improvements to the Blast. He always had some new design ideas he wanted to test.

I stopped behind Ray, wondering what I could do to help. But the sentries motioned me on. They were still treating me like a big threat, so I kept moving.

The SensEye swiveled and followed me. Its metal casing blinked like a human eye, and the raspy click made the hair on the back of my neck prickle. This SensEye was smaller than a human head, but it was still intimidating. I could hear the lens constantly adjusting focus. I hate being watched. The interrogator behind me shouted, "Well?" and I jumped a bit.

I heard Ray answer. "Well, when she passed through the detection gates, there weren't any pilot alerts, either." He was talking about me. The SensEye swiveled back around to focus on him again. I could hear it. And I glanced back to see, too. The bands on his forearms lit up. Several rows of yellow circled his wrists, and he looked alarmed. Each row of light meant an infraction, and their effect was cumulative. I saw him wince in pain.

"Stop hurting him!" I said, "He didn't know. He couldn't have known." I couldn't let the man be punished for something I'd done. Especially not someone who wore a band. His class was always punished for the slightest infraction.

He winced again, and I blurted, "I didn't set off an alert because I used a science officer universal access code." As much as I wanted to hold onto the fake identification and all the access it provided me, I pulled the triangular-shaped chip from my inside tunic pocket.

The interrogator eyed the chip, and I flipped it to him. He said, "You passed through the gate with this?"

"Yes." There it was, plain and simple, my full confession. And now the officials knew how I'd managed—without detection—to get off deck for an unauthorized test flight. I expected the yellow infraction lights on the innocent crewman's band to dim. But they didn't.

Instead the interrogator held the fake chip in Ray's face. "You let her trick you—with this?"

A very small man wearing a tall, cylindrical hat strutted out of a black doorway. His hat indicated he held a high rank in the security force. He was an MP, a Master Patrolman. "Virginia Bosque" he barked, "Sit." I sat where he pointed on the interrogation bench, a full meter away from the others.

The MP took the orange summons disk from one of the escort sentries and flicked through my record. He had this annoying facial tic: one of his nostrils twitched. Finally, he stepped toward me until he was almost on top of my toes and looked at me in a way that unnerved me more than the SensEye. "Maureen Bosque was your mother?"

Was?! I hated it when anyone talked about my mother as if she were dead. She was officially considered missing. Through clenched teeth I answered, "She is."

The MP rose slightly on his heels and pivoted. "Not only did you deviate from your flight plan, you are not even registered to fly the Galaxy . . ." He checked the summons disk and flicked it several times. "What's the model?"

I supplied the information he couldn't find. "It's a Blast."

"Repeat, you are NOT registered to fly the Galaxy Blast on Test Flight E100 or any other flight plan," the MP said.

"Of course, she's not," Dot said. "She's not registered to pilot the craft in question for the flight in question, because she does not yet have her pilot's license."

"Whose side are you on?" I whispered. Even though Dot was only stating a fact the security team could easily check, I felt betrayed.

"Impound the little Galaxy model," the MP ordered the two sentries, and they scurried away.

"You can't impound my Blast! My dad gave it to me for my birthday!" But, of course, none of the men paid any attention to me. I said to Dot, "See what you did."

Then the MP growled, "This girl isn't authorized to take any ship off deck." He kept flicking through the file on the summons disk. "She's barely old enough to get a learner's permit." He sounded surprised, as if he'd just figured out my age and how that factored into the situation. He turned on Ray. "Why didn't you check her pilot's authorization?"

"Ah." Ray glanced up at me, and then slumped even lower on the bench. "She seemed to know what she was doing."

The interrogator logged another infraction on Ray's light band. "Failure to cross-check full authorization."

Another row of yellow lit Ray's wrist and his eyes watered. I wasn't getting the zap, but just seeing it happen to someone else made my skin feel hot.

I hadn't meant to get him into trouble with my clever use of a fake ID chip and a security loophole big enough to fly a scramjet through. Zap. I knew he wouldn't suffer permanent damage. But I also knew it hurt. I couldn't imagine how badly he felt.

"Still think your test flight was worth the risk?" Dot asked.

I never intended for anyone else to be punished for my actions, but I wasn't willing to accept all the responsibility. I said, "You could have gotten us out of this." And I folded her face flap down.

A shrill whistle announced something. Most likely something unpleasant. The MP said, "Stand," and he pointed at a security transmission screen dropping from the ceiling.

The standard triangular logo of the Triumvirate Corporation faded out and next on screen was—not good—my dad. He was wearing his official jacket, the one with the high, tight collar. That meant he was going to or coming from a high-pressure meeting, and whatever I might need would only be an added irritation. This time the interruption hadn't been my idea, and there was nothing I could do but explain the situation. "Dad, first of all, they're punishing an innocent man. Second of all, they took my Blast."

"Virginia," he sighed in that what-have-you-done-now tone of voice. He looked at the MP and said, "You called?"

"Yes, sir," the MP answered crisply. "Is this your daughter?"

"If you mean, do we have a 50% DNA match? Yes," Dad hated explaining basic genetics. "Is that why you called?"

The MP looked from my dad to me, and back again. I knew the MP saw my dad's pale skin, an extreme contrast to my own skin color, what Dad called *sweet caramel*. So, I explained, "I look like my mother."

"Sir." The MP obviously heard but ignored me. "Did you see the memo I sent about your daughter's infraction?

"No." Dad's eyebrows bristled. "But I assume that's why you're calling me now, interrupting a demonstration of my new design for faster-than-light communication."

I had considerable experience interrupting Dad when he was demonstrating one of his inventions, and it had never turned out well for me. In an odd way, I felt sorry for the scrawny MP. It wasn't going to turn out well for him either, despite his badge of authority.

The MP cleared his throat and continued, "The craft in question—which, according to financial records, you purchased—is unaccountably NOT in the transit system registry. I've sent the Galaxy to Impound."

"Yes, understood. I'll be sure to take care of the registration before my daughter earns her license and is officially authorized to pilot her own craft." Then my dad gave me his most disapproving look.

"Sir," said the MP "The problem is, sir, she's already been flying without a license."

Dad's eyes locked with the MP's. "Your crew let my child off deck? Without a license?" Though Dad spoke gently, the MP's cheeks blazed with the accusation. Dad continued, "Then the problem is in your security system, is it not?" He let the full impact of his words sink in. "If her infraction and those of the flight crew who let her off deck were to be entered into the permanent log, it would point back to your failure."

Now the MP looked alarmed. My dad continued in an even softer voice, "Might I suggest that without an official record of the problem, there will have been no problem." When it came to negotiating with security types, my dad had a way with words.

The MP pocketed the orange summons disk and bowed in agreement, "Sir." He adjusted his stiff collar and forced a smile.

Leave it to my dad to know how to take advantage of bureaucratic paranoia. The security officers didn't want to be in trouble, so that meant I got off easy.

Dad worked the system a little more. "I further suggest leaving the craft in Impound—the safest place for all concerned—but that you forego all the security notices, as well as any light band enforcements you may have felt were necessary for crew discipline."

Of course, I wasn't happy about Dad's keep-the-Blast-in-Impound suggestion. But I was relieved he thought of the crewman, especially someone who couldn't have been much older than me. Almost immediately, the young man's light band dimmed and he started to breath normally again.

I sucked in a big gulp of air. I hadn't realized I'd been holding my breath.

"I'll make sure we won't run into this kind of difficulty again." Dad looked at me. "Virginia?"

I suppose Dad wanted me to verify that I wouldn't jump ship again. I was grateful that my top-scientist dad knew how to work around security protocols. I was especially grateful he stopped the innocent crewman's punishment. But still, I wasn't entirely satisfied. "Dad, what about my Blast?" As soon as the words were out of my mouth, I knew I'd pushed beyond his limit.

Dad's gaze turned to titanium. "We'll discuss this later. Now, you're confined to quarters." And he signed off.

Being sent to quarters may sound harsh, but it's a lot better than lockdown. Trust me.

⊕

Confined to Quarters

All the way to K-Deck, where I live, I obsessed about how close I was to earning my license. Had I lost future flying privileges? If so, for how long? Dad had convinced the MP to leave my unauthorized flight off the permanent log, but I had no idea what penalties or delays Dad might impose. Inside our family quarters the first thing I did was flop on my sleeping sofa and bury my face into Dot's soft side.

It may sound like I was seeking comfort from my PIRSD again. To clarify, I never did, and never will, call my Personal Information Retrieval and Storage Device a "pirsd" out loud. It sounds vulgar. Her name is Dot. And, yes, I was seeking comfort from her. I always do and always had, since my earliest memories. Comfort-giving is one of her finest design features.

Dot's more than a standard PIRSD tutor. She's a TODD model, a Transportable and Omniscient Data Device. In other words, she knows everything. Plus, she's custom engineered by my dad, so everything about her is the best in the galaxy. Her main interface is the special flex-form I wear wrapped around my forearm everywhere

I go. She's not bulky, more like a long sleeve. And for quick access, I can open one corner with a touch.

TODD sounds like a boy's name, so I flipped the initials and named her Dot, after her plush and cuddly polka-dotted cover where I rested my cheek.

"Wake up, Dot. I need you." I opened her corner face flap on the inside of my wrist.

Dot opened her eyes lazily. Her smooth screen side is fireproof and waterproof, virtually indestructible. And once she's open, her eyes take on different visual qualities depending on her mood. So when I describe her eyes as *lazy*, I mean at that particular time they looked like they were painted with a brush and the movements were slow and flowing.

"Is it already time for another *Dear Dot* log?" She yawned and added, "As I recall, our last entry was fairly extravagant. You remember all that unauthorized flight footage I attached." She was playing her languid diva persona. "The pictures are stunning, if I do say so myself."

"Yes, Dot. The pictures are stunning. No, I didn't wake you to make another log entry. It's time for an action plan." I was done with pouting. I was ready to act on my personal mission. "How am I going to get my Blast out of Impound?"

"Getting your Blast out of Impound won't automatically get you back in the pilot's seat." She yawned again.

"Dot, I'm going crazy trying to figure out what to do."

"Focus," Dot shifted to her tutoring tone of voice and, to match her attitude, the lines defining her eyes grew thin and straight. "To solve any complicated problem, simply focus on the first step."

And the first step was what? Dot always did this. She left out the difficult part and expected me to figure it out. For as she would explain: After the struggle is when real learning occurs. Sometimes, like this one, I didn't want to learn. I just wanted to fly. That's all I'd ever wanted. But I couldn't explore the galaxy if I couldn't even leave my quarters. "I'm trapped, Dot."

"Leo will not make you stay here forever," she said.

Even though Dot always called my dad by his first name, Leo, this time just hearing his name in a casual way made my temperature shoot up. She was clearly in league with parental enforcement, no matter what she said with her soothing words. "Even two minutes is too long!" I paced frantically, back and forth, a handful of steps in each direction.

"Tranquillo, hot-sauce." That was Dot's way of telling me to calm down.

But I embraced my hormonal self. "I'm totally justified!" I wasn't. "I wouldn't be confined to quarters if it weren't for you. You could have helped me avoid detection when we landed."

"You're blaming me?" Dot sounded incredulous.

I knew I wasn't being logical, but I continued to shout, "You're right. I'd rather blame my mother for everything that's wrong. But you know, she's uber-unavailable. I'd like to blame Daddio. But he might as well be lost in space, too." I was being completely unfair. Dad had actually helped me out of a tight spot, but once I'd launched into a tirade, it was impossible to stop.

"Virginia." Dot's voice took on her most soothing tone, weighted with a hint of disappointment.

"Fine." I stood with my hands on my hips, arms akimbo. Obviously, I wasn't ready to let go of the blame game.

"I detect excess energy." Searching her vast database, which extended to all recorded human history, including fictional history, Dot called up a personality that would make me smile. Her eyes shifted into something silver. "This isn't personal." She sounded like one of my favorite 20th Century cinema characters, a cyborg with an Austrian accent. "I detect a perfect opportunity for you to focus in a productive manner. Time for a workout."

I grumbled but I knew Dot, a.k.a. The Terminator, was right. So I shed my outer tunic and tied my straight hair into a knot to keep it out of my face. I unwrapped Dot from my forearm and spread her out on her refreshing station. Then I snapped on my moon boots, set the gravity control on them, and walked up the wall and across the ceiling.

Oops. My amber pendant bonked me on the nose. I slipped it over my head, twisted awkwardly, and reached to set it on top of the clear display case. Somehow, I managed to bump the case with my funny bone. "Ouch." Inside the case an eagle feather—as in the last eagle feather in existence, a priceless artifact—swayed gently from the bump. I watched it to make sure the feather was all right. It looked completely undamaged.

I moved a few steps over where there was room enough to exercise, did three sets of ab curls, and then kept going until I couldn't curl up any more. Finally my body relaxed. There I was, hanging upside-down and gazing out the window the way I always did after a workout.

I'd seen these star patterns countless times, but now I was intensely aware of how different it was when I'd seen the same points of light from the cockpit of my Blast. It was more than the view. In deep space I wasn't confined to simulator routines.

I closed my eyes, remembering what it felt like. The best was when I flew as fast as I could and turned as tightly as I could starboard, raced back, crossing my own flight path, and turned portside, then raced again across my own path, carving a figure eight over and over again. I tagged the new move the *infinity chase*, even though I wasn't chasing anyone but myself.

The faster I flew, the quieter everything seemed.

My mind grew calm.

Still.

Then Gordy burst in, bringing me back to the present, and our cramped quarters. "Hey, Gin Gin, where've you been?"

Typical Gordy, ruining a perfect, peaceful moment. My hair unraveled and hung down over my head.

"Come on. I need . . ." Gordy didn't finish his sentence. He had this annoying habit of stopping in the middle of sentences, especially when it was something important.

"What do you need this time?" Even when he was annoying—which was most of the time—I wanted to know what was going on. Gordy is my younger cousin. His parents were lost in space and had been out of the picture since he was a baby. So my dad was the parent figure in his life, and we grew up like siblings sharing just about everything.

He blurted his answer, "It's on Z-Deck."

Dot and I had planned to meet Gordy on Z-Deck, but that was before the whole lockdown experience. Obviously my plans had been rearranged. I still didn't know what he wanted, but Z-Deck was the place I needed to be. I had a plan to get back into my pilot's seat. "Perfect. I need to go to Z-Deck to earn my license."

"I heard you didn't need a license to get off deck." He grinned.

"How did you know?" I lunged at him.

He stepped out of my reach. "Gin Gin." With a handheld device he changed the gravity control settings on my boots and I dropped to the floor.

"You beast!" I grabbed, but he kept side stepping away. Even though he was only 12, he was almost as big as me, so physically we were a fair match. I finally managed to snag the hem of his pant leg. In the struggle we slammed into the pedestal that supported the display case holding the precious eagle feather. The whole thing tumbled over, and the clear case cracked open on the floor.

"Zap," Gordy and I said, at the same time.

The feather came loose and floated up a bit, and I held my breath. For as long as I could remember I'd looked at the artifact inside the case, but I'd never touched it. I caught the feather in my open palms. It felt so soft, and I felt so protective.

I said, "This was my mother's."

"I've heard." Gordy didn't sound sympathetic. His attention wasn't even on the feather. He was looking inside the now horizontal pedestal base. "Was this hers, too?" He pulled at something big lodged inside the base. Even though it was twice his size around and over half as long as he was tall, he managed to pull a strange cargo container partway out.

The container was made of the best metal alloy, very modern but with the retro style of an old ocean-going steamer trunk. I wrapped my hair back up and stuck the feather in the knot to get everything out of the way and free up my hands, and helped pull the object free.

"A treasure chest," Gordy said.

I blurted, "That's ridiculous."

Gordy looked wounded. He always looked wounded when I sounded critical of him, which I frequently was—not a fact that I'm proud of, but apparently it's my nature.

I turned my attention to our discovery. Not even in my wildest dreams had I thought of finding any kind of treasure, much less a family treasure. But here it was, a hidden chest, covered with textured patterns.

Clearly it was a precious object and, considering the weight, quite possibly filled with more precious objects. I touched the engraved name—Bosque, our family name, passed from mother to daughter—and I wondered when the chest had been packed. Mostly, I wanted to know what was inside. "Can you open it?" Gordy was really good at picking locks.

He nodded, pulled a small tool out of his pocket, and tried to wedge it into the seam. "This is . . ." He shook his head. There didn't seem to be any way to get into the trunk.

"Don't give up so easily," I said.

"Zap," he said, clearly discouraged. "Sorry, Gin. I don't want . . ."

I guessed he was afraid he might damage the chest. "I agree, we shouldn't force the lock. Take your time. You'll get it."

The lights in our quarters dimmed to the nighttime setting. It was later than I thought. Gordy flicked on a flashlight and aimed it at the lock so he could continue. The beam cast shadows along the side of the textured chest, revealing more of the intricate engraving.

"Gordy, I think there's something more here than beautiful decoration." I ran my fingertips along the seam to confirm the pattern I recognized, this one etched in the metal. I'd be a total failure if I didn't know what a star chart looked and felt like. My entire teenage life was wrapped around intensive navigation studies. "Someone has triangulated a particular location." Finding the precise coordinates, I touched the stars. "Here, here, and here." The chest opened with a gentle pop.

⊕

The Family Treasure Chest

When the lid popped open, I just sat there, too excited to think what to do. Gordy lifted the lid and let it fall back, revealing the contents of the treasure chest. A calming scent filled the room, and I gazed at the neat stacks of folded cloth, noticing vivid colors and an unbelievable variety of textures inviting my touch. What were these things? Should we treat them like archeological artifacts? Only to be handled with precise scientific protocol?

Gordy seemed just as mesmerized by our discovery. He leaned over the open chest and breathed deeply. "I'd like to crawl in and dream."

Dot said, "You are responding to the smell of lavender, known for its relaxing effect on humans. The dried flowers of the lavender plant are used to keep fabric fresh, so you will likely find packets of lavender placed among the contents of the chest." Leave it to Dot to explain the facts behind everything.

I continued with her logic. If whoever stored the fabric inside the chest intended to keep it fresh, then these things were meant to be used again. So, I pulled out one piece after another of the most fabulous clothes. Unlike the standard blue tunic and pant sets we always wore, these clothes were built from flowing fabrics in all the colors of the prism. Gordy joined me, and before long every surface inside our quarters was festooned with wild shapes and textures.

When he was little Gordy loved to play dress-up and, once he started tying on sashes, I was inspired, draping scarves around my neck and across my arms. My favorite was a fluttering, lace shawl. Gordy found a rich, velvet robe and he posed like a king of ancient times.

Ridiculous? Childish? We were alone in our quarters. Who knew?

I gravitated back to the chest to explore more of the treasure, and touched a shimmering sea-green dress.

"Did your mother wear that?" he asked.

"I don't remember. I don't remember any of them." But who else would have stored the clothes in our quarters? I held the dress close to my body and tried to imagine the person who had worn it. It was a little big. I wondered if I'd grow into it.

Gordy dug into the bottom of the trunk, and pulled out a pair of embroidered shoes. "Maybe my mother wore some of them, too." I'd never heard him talk about his mother. He didn't remember her, so it didn't come up. But the clothes were tangible evidence of the mothers we'd lost. He slid his toes in, but his heels hung over the back of the flats.

Underneath everything I found something that looked very old. Dot called it a silk kimono. I expected it to be light and flowing like the other clothes, but when I picked it up, it was heavy. Wrapped inside it I found a large book, which looked even older. I set it aside. I was more interested in feeling the weight of the silk, and I slipped the kimono on.

While I twirled and the loose sleeves fluttered around me, Gordy knelt down and opened the book. I understood his reverence. Physical books were rare and this one was very unusual. "Look," he called to me.

I spun to the floor, and he pointed to page after page of beautifully rendered paintings of plants. Each included a description of its edibility, medicinal use, and method of propagation.

Gordy turned back to the front of the book and examined the inscription inside the cover. The tiny handwriting was meticulous. That I could tell. He bent closer to the page. "This book was made by a Planetary Protection Officer, Vera Bosque." Gordy whispered, "Gin. She was our great-great-great-great-great-grandmother."

"You're stuttering."

Gordy shook his head and said firmly, "Our five times great-grandmother."

"As in as in five generations ago?"

"Technically, seven."

"Five greats." I held up five fingers.

"Plus one regular gran."

"Plus our moms." I added the sixth and seventh fingers.

Gordy nodded. "This book was made in pre-colonization times." He whispered, "Gin, she lived on Earth." He pointed to the handwritten preface.

Underneath the title, *Edible and Medicinal Plant Life of Earth,* I read Vera's words out loud, "I have purposely chosen to copy all available knowledge by hand so that it cannot be in any way modified by on-line censors." I picked up the large illuminated manuscript, weighing the knowledge.

"Zap!" Gordy said, "Great-gran Vera was in the resistance." He pointed at the stamped seal on the bottom of the page. It was an emblem of the E.R.A., the Earth Restoration Alliance. Gordy took the book and turned the page, reading Great-gran Vera's introduction.

We knew something about the secret Alliance. Everyone did. But, it was tough to piece together the scraps of information. There were just enough stories to wonder what might have been, if members of the Alliance had been the ones to take control instead of the Triumvirate. Here was evidence that our ancestor had been part of the resistance movement.

Gordy said, "Her book contains the life secrets of our planet."

"Our planet? Earth's been dead for generations," I said.

"Let's show it to Dot," Gordy said.

"You mean scan the whole thing? That would take forever. What would be the point?"

"News flash, genius. Our gran's talking about bringing life *back* to Earth."

"Gotcha, Gordo. That's *everybody's* old dream. And no book can make that happen." I took off the kimono, folded it along with all the other finery, and carefully replaced the things inside the chest. I was done playing with old things.

Gordy wasn't. He was still infatuated with the heavily textured paper of the book. He traced the beautiful lettering with his fingers and discovered, between the title page and the preface, a pocket. "Gin"

I didn't want to talk anymore. Not about the kind of wishful thinking that just made people feel dissatisfied. Earth was a lost cause. Any energy spent in that direction was a waste.

"Gin Gin, look." Gordy pulled a piece of paper from the slim pocket inside the manuscript. He held the paper up. It was a letter addressed to me.

Gently, I took the letter. Unlike the paper in Greatgran Vera's illuminated manuscript, the texture was smooth. The small, folded pages were tied with a piece of green ribbon. I looked at the handwriting, large and loopy. All that was written on the outside was my name, Virginia Bosque. The dots over each 'i' were tiny swirls. A heart sat inside the letter "V." Whoever had written my name had made it special. It looked so familiar.

Gordy asked, "What's it say?"

I slid the ribbon off and opened the pages. I read, "Dearest Virginia, If you find this note, then I have missed the joy of watching you grow up. I passionately hope not, but it is a sad possibility I must risk. As much as missing your birthdays and your countless triumphs—for I already know that you excel in so many ways—I apologize for failing to accomplish the mission entrusted to our family for generations. It now falls on you, as next in line, to recover microscopic plant life from the oceans of Green Tara and carry them back to Earth."

Gordy jumped up. "She's talking about the legend."

I handed the first page to Gordy and continued, "You will find the information you need in Vera's manuscript. Your destiny is to restore life to our home planet." No pressure in that. Zap. I was still confined to quarters. How could I save a planet?

"Green Tara! Gin, the legend of Green Tara." Gordy thought we'd discovered the clues to that ridiculous old dream. "What else does she say?"

I skipped over the signature and read the last line, "P.S. I left the propagation catalyst with Dot."

"What?" asked Gordy.

I wasn't sure what she meant by that last line either, but my focus jumped from the postscript back up to the way the letter was signed. It said, *I love you and I wish we could do this together, Momo.*

Momo. When I was a little girl, that's what I called my mother. Momo.

Gordy whispered, "What if the chance to bring life back to Earth is more than a dream?"

I shoved the letter into my tunic. I couldn't save a planet. Not alone. Not without Momo. She couldn't do it either. "Forget it."

"We can't just forget it, Gin. She's talking about the mission to restore life on Earth." Gordy said, "That's what your mother was doing when she was lost."

Now Gordy was so excited he was talking in complete sentences. I just shook my head.

"Lost? She didn't just simply get lost, Gordo. Didn't you hear what she said? My mother left me to go on an impossible dream. She got herself lost." I was trying to hold it together, like this was old news, but big fat tears sprung to my eyes.

Gordy sat next to the chest. "Gin, if the pattern etched on the chest is a star chart, maybe it points to a particular place."

"You mean, Green Tara?"

He nodded. "Now we have the clues to find it, and maybe your mother."

If Gordy was right, and we had found the coordinates to Momo's last known location ... Wait. Where had my mother gotten her information? And how accurate could a star chart to a legendary planet be? After all, she hadn't come back from her mission. She'd left me to find a place that *might* exist.

I looked at the beautiful fabrics and breathed in the lovely scent, but the lavender wasn't enough to make me feel calm. My stomach churned. I couldn't take any more reminders about what I'd lost. I dropped the lid and snapped the chest closed. The air inside our quarters was suffocating. I had to get out. After all, Dad hadn't specifically said how long I had to stay confined.

I picked up Dot—she was glowing again—and wrapped her around my arm in travel mode.

I told Gordy, "Hide the chest in your room."

"Where are you going?" Gordy asked.

Without thinking it through, instinctively I knew my next destination. I answered, "To Z-Deck."

"Good." Gordy said, "I have something to show you."

"Your show and tell has to wait. I'm going to Navigation," I said.

"To Navigation?" His face lit up. "So you can follow the star chart your mother left us?"

"Gordy, take a sanity pill." I pointed to the chest, "This star chart is clearly an unreliable navigational tool. We don't know if my mother even made it to Green Tara. She sure didn't make it back. And let's remember that Green Tara is a *legendary*—as in fictional—terrestrial planet."

"Maybe," Gordy whispered. "But maybe it's the real deal."

"It's not real!" I wasn't trying to hurt his feelings. It was just–I didn't believe anything was real, not in the sense that a person could count on it forever. Even the stars aren't permanent. Sure, they're real for as long as they last, but they aren't eternal. They flame and die out.

The only thing that felt real to me was flying. I wanted to fly again, and fly just for the fun of it. I was not aiming for a doom and gloom destination of lost dreams.

I had to focus.

I had to have a license for Dad to even consider getting my Blast out of impound and letting me back into the pilot's seat. And I knew exactly what I needed to do to earn it.

I headed for the door.

Gordy called, "Gin Gin?" He sounded forlorn. I was obviously going without him. "Why are you going to Navigation?"

"To earn my pilot's license."

⊕

⊕

My Pilot's License

Gordy followed me, as usual. To catch up he sprinted down the corridor to the transport tube, all the way bombarding me with questions. "How can you earn your pilot's license? You're not …"

"…old enough?" I countered. "Dad's always saying maturity and skill are not tied to chronological age."

"Yes, but how…?

I stepped inside the tube and gave my destination. "Z-Deck."

Gordy slipped in beside me. "Z-Deck?

The pneumatic door sucked shut. "All I have left is my qualifying exam. I'm sure it will be easy enough for me to pass." I snapped a safety harness on, and motioned for Gordy to do the same. "Then Dad can file my pilot's application."

"Uncle Leo can't …"

"Get around the rules? Dad bends the rules all the time." The transport tube started to move, instantly forcing enormous pressure on my knees and every other part of my body. I strained to keep speaking while the tube shot from K-Deck to Z-Deck. "I've already proven my flying skills in the simulator *and* in real flight time. I'm mature for my age. Everyone says so. And, I'm being groomed to lead science expeditions. Remember? That's how I was categorized on my personal record. Clearly, I need more flying experience. Multiple reasons for Dad to file for a variance on the minimum age rule for pilot licenses."

"Maybe," Gordy shrugged, but he didn't argue the point. As the tube began to slow, he asked another annoying question. "What's on the qualifying exam?"

"It's all about navigation. Advanced skills. What you have to know if you ever need to re-chart your course."

Gordy said, "It'll be easy for you to chart the way from here to Green Tara."

"No," I said. "That's not the plan. The plan is to qualify for my license."

"You can find and rescue your mother." He sounded so enthusiastic about a mission that was destined to fail. "You have to try."

"No, I don't." There's no teenage rulebook that says rescue of long-lost mothers is a requirement.

Phshht. The pneumatic pressure released at the stop. We both unbuckled, and the tube door flew open, dropping us directly into the most elegant location onboard our colonial cruiser.

This was Navigation—the expansive, triangular-shaped bay in the forward prow. Floor-to-ceiling windows stretched over the two outward-facing walls of the bay. A mosaic of screens filled the inside wall, and on each screen was a different view of the galaxy. Everywhere you looked there were stars. Without a doubt, Navigation was one of my favorite places onboard.

In addition to the sheer beauty, Navigation was distinctive for what was absent. There were no SensEyes hovering about. Something about their communication protocols created interference in the navigation instruments—an obvious safety hazard—so SensEyes simply could not be inside the Navigation Bay.

No one was watching.

That little bit of tightness in my chest let go, and I breathed easily. Even the air in Navigation smelled sweeter.

The bay was nearly empty. The only people were the Chief of Navigation and a couple of assistants. I crossed to a familiar work station, shushed Gordy, who was still right behind me, and spread Dot out on the training console.

"This is not a good idea," said Dot in her most prim nanny mode.

These constant interruptions were wearing me down. I opened the qualifying exam on the console.

Dot continued, "Not only have you ignored the directive your father gave you to stay in our quarters, I must remind you that the Chief of Navigation told you not to return to take the qualifying exam until *after* you received authorization."

Gordy said to Dot, "She thinks the rules apply to someone else."

"I'm not violating any rule by taking the exam now. The Chief meant it would be better for me to get prior authorization. It was, in his opinion, a better use of my time," I said.

"The Chief has *opinions* forged by many years of experience, and you would do well to value his perspective and advice." Dot stared at me with her steeliest look.

"If he doesn't want me here, he'll ask me to leave." I knew the Chief wouldn't mind. He was another reason I liked this bay above every other location on board. He taught me my favorite subject in a way that made every problem a game. It always started with where did I want to go, and why? Pick a star. Any star. And then the question was how would I get there?

In addition to tutoring me in navigation skills, it was the Chief's job to advise me. He had. And I had made the decision to complete my testing requirements ahead of time, knowing that technically I wasn't old enough for a pilot's license, and I would still have to deal with the age variance issue and official authorization. But I'd been trained to take problems one step at a time. I smiled back at Dot and focused on the open exam.

Gordy tried to get my attention. "Gin."

"Don't." I didn't look up. I was trying to concentrate.

Gordy circled away to another area of the bay, giving me the peace I needed to do my work.

My focus stayed on the navigation problems in front of me. But in the middle of my third and last problem I overheard Gordy asking the Chief to put the planet Earth on display. I thought Gordy's new obsession was silly. But I heard the Chief's gravelly voice. "Interesting choice, Earth."

I turned around to see what the Chief, the master navigator of the ship, would call up on the orb. He tapped a code on his directional wand and pointed it up to the projection system. "Let's take a look." The orb shimmered as he set up its three-dimensional image.

I rushed to finish my computations. After all, the central navigation orb was the most glorious object on board. Although calling it an object was not accurate in the strictest sense of the word. The orb wasn't matter—solid, liquid, or gas. It was the focal point of star chart and planetary imaging, and I didn't want to miss anything.

Just as I completed the exam, the orb hummed. I looked up again and watched it go pure white. Even from across the bay, I recognized the atmospheric clouds and I wanted to get a closer look. So I asked Dot to send my exam to the master key for evaluation and headed for the center of the bay.

As I approached the orb, the clouds parted to reveal a planet of swirling blue water and vibrant green land. Even though I'd seen Earth in countless history lessons, it was still fascinating to look at a living, dynamic biosphere.

The Chief, a white-haired man even older than my dad, said, "Virginia, I trust you recognize our prime terra." He motioned for me to come closer. "You'll enjoy this, too."

I stepped up on the circular platform that ringed the orb and looked at the velvety Earth. This was the planet where my ancestors had come from, the birthplace of our species.

The orb projected more than the geological outlines of the continents. The detail was amazing. I could see vegetation, the self-regulating engines that use photosynthesis to convert sun energy to food and oxygen. Theoretically plants are fascinating. And here I saw that "chlorophyll" green wasn't just one flat, uniform color. There were countless variations, from a bright, almost yellow hue to a cool, deep blue green. The colors and rich textures were so inviting that I reached out to touch them, but of course my fingers went right through the projected image.

The Chief said, "That's the Amazon Rain Forest. Of course, this is an historical map. Let's look at the current state." He squeezed the wand. The shape of the continents remained basically the same, though somewhat smaller, but the texture of the land changed dramatically. Almost all of the plant life withered and blew away. The land surface hardened, and all the colors faded to gray. "An inactive biosphere."

"Dead?" Gordy knew the facts, so he wasn't asking as much as contemplating Earth's fate.

"Not absolutely dead. Some life forms don't need oxygen or water. But for human needs," the Chief shook his head and said, "the atmosphere is beyond repair."

He'd given a straightforward description of Earth's biosphere, the same description I'd always heard. But I detected a sense of irony, as if there was more the Chief knew that he was unwilling to share.

"Now, for an interesting comparison, let's jump across the galaxy and look at a multi-star view." The Chief reset the wand, and the scattered stars of deep space appeared. One bright blue spot represented our ship, and a spiraling arc represented our flight path curving through the space. "This is our current location and course. This is where we'll be tomorrow." With a flick of his wrist he pointed to one edge, and the ship moved along our plotted course.

Our ship, the colonial cruiser, looked the same. What changed radically was the space to the port side of our course. Gone were the glittering points of light from distant suns. Instead, that side of the orb glared orange.

"Ew-w-w. Orange space," Gordy said.

"It's not orange space. We're looking at a mask." I whispered, "The Forbidden Zone." I'd studied the zone, but I'd never seen it displayed.

The Chief gazed into the harsh orange light and grumbled something about environmental hazards, the risk of contamination, and preventing the spread of infectious diseases.

The sarcastic tone of his voice was unmistakable now. Clearly the Chief was withholding information. But why? He'd always been generous and thorough with his knowledge. Like Dot, the Chief had taught me to ask the difficult questions. His favorite line was: Only difficult questions lead to interesting truth.

So, what was the difficult question in front of us now? I understood that the Zone was marked a nasty orange to indicate a quarantined area, and that access to it, like everything in the galaxy, was strictly controlled by the Triumvirate Corporation. I voiced the obvious—not-so-difficult when you think about it—question, "And the reason we can't see into the Zone . . . ? Chief, help us out here. It's not logical. Viewing the Zone won't contaminate us."

"Spatial information for the Forbidden Zone is blocked for *safety* reasons," the Chief answered. He stepped off the orb platform to accept a message disc delivered by the apprentice navigator, and moved to the communication panel on the back wall.

"Safety reasons?" I wasn't satisfied with the lame explanation, but the Chief was clearly done explaining. This was so unlike him. I'd never heard him use the 'safety' excuse, like my other teachers and mentors. The Chief always pointed out when Triumvirate regulations were conflicting or senseless. Whenever something was against the rules *for safety reasons,* I knew that was a generic label for irrational Triumvirate control.

In this kind of situation, typically, the Chief would have demonstrated a system work-around so he could navigate according to logic. But apparently, the Forbidden Zone was forbidden enough to keep out even the Chief Navigator. I muttered, "I still don't understand the point of the orange mask."

The orb light dimmed, so that the image was still visible but not nearly as bright.

The apprentice was still standing by and he must have heard my question. He took a step toward me and whispered. "The official explanation is that the Zone is uninhabitable. Dangerous. The Triumvirate forbids passage." The new apprentice sounded familiar. I glanced at his name tag—"Ray"—and caught his gaze. I knew those eyes, flecked with green and gold. This was the same young man who was punished in lockdown for my unauthorized flight.

I sucked in air. "Did you get reassigned?"

He bowed formally and whispered, "Your joy ride cost me an uncomfortable hour, but now I have the best assignment on board." He grinned.

"That was fast." Apparently the MP in lockdown took my dad's directions very seriously.

"The moment you left, they banned me from the flight deck," he said, "And they warned me not to ever talk about the incident involving your Blast."

"Then let's not talk about it." I was embarrassed about being in lockdown, so I was relieved the topic was off limits. But something else he said struck a nerve. "Back up to what you said about the Zone being uninhabitable. You said that was the 'official explanation?' As in, not the whole story?"

"I've heard some ideas." He glanced around. I presume he was checking to see who might be listening. No one. Except Gordy, of course.

Ray said, "It's just another way for the Triumvirate to control resources, isn't it?" He understood.

I said, "I've never seen the Chief react so strongly to anything."

We all looked at the opaque orange mask that dominated the orb.

"I don't have any hard facts about why the Zone was established," Ray said.

"It must be a political block," Gordy said. "Or, there's something valuable to hide in ..."

"Gordy, don't jump to conclusions," I interrupted, because I wasn't sure if we could trust Ray. Sure, we shared an unusual experience. But this was the first time we'd actually exchanged any thoughts. He could easily be a corporate spy, a sort of human SensEye, placed in our midst to test our loyalty. I certainly didn't want anyone to suspect Gordy of RTP, resistance to policy. The authorities might attach monitors to him, even if he was just a kid.

Ray laughed and continued Gordy's line of thought. "So the question is, what's so valuable inside the Zone that it's blocked from passage *and* from view? I've heard pirates prowl the Zone looking for treasure." Ray bared his teeth, playing scary. "Dangerous pirates."

"Another *safety* reason to stay out of the Zone?" My sarcastic remark just slipped out. Oops.

"Yes, of course," said Ray. "The blockade is for our safety. We all know *the Triumvirate's most noble purpose is to keep the population safe from exposure to any potentially negative contact.*" Even though Ray quoted from the constitutional incorporation contract, he sounded cynical. In a completely different tone of voice, he spoke directly to me, softly. "I'm glad to see you again, here in Navigation."

I hated the fact he knew confidential information about me and refused to encourage any kind of ongoing friendship. I snapped, "I'm simply here because I need to earn my license."

"I heard you didn't need a license to get off deck." His smile broadened.

Gordy poked me in the ribs and I slapped his hand away.

"I heard that, too," boomed the Chief.

Did everybody on board the ship know about my unauthorized test flight?

The Chief tapped Ray on the shoulder and handed the message disc back to him. Ray bowed to the Chief, and then to me—to Gordy, too, I suppose—and left the bay.

I glared at Gordy, but he completely ignored me. Meanwhile, the Chief joined us on the orb platform and reset the wand.

The murky Forbidden Zone floated brightly in front of us again. Gordy tried to blow away the haze obscuring the stars and planets. "Come on, Chief," he said. "No one else is here in the bay now. I think there may be terrestrial planets in there. Let's see, please."

"Unfortunately, I have no charts of planets inside the Zone," said the Chief.

"We have information about a planet. A description," said Gordy.

The Chief asked, "Inside the Zone?"

Certainly Gordy knew our family chest held secrets that we should keep, well, secret. Great-gran Vera's manuscript had been hidden for generations. Wait. I tried to get his attention, but he was ignoring me.

"What planet? And how do you know about it?" The Chief sounded surprised.

"Virginia's mother went into the Zone," Gordy said. "That's where she disappeared."

"That's wild speculation, Gordo. This whole thing about the legend and my mother has gotten completely out of control," I said.

"Perhaps not. Perhaps Gordy is right." The Chief's voice dropped to a whisper. "The last time our flight path brought us adjacent to the Zone was ten years ago. Your mother was able to shift the orange mask."

"My mother?" "You knew my mother?" Nausea threatened to overtake me.

"Yes, I did. Before you, Virginia, your mother was my greatest navigation student." He gazed into my eyes. "She had the same clear vision you have."

I blinked and looked away. The Chief had never mentioned my mother before. I looked at the opaque security mask that blocked everyone's sensors. "Are you saying that my mother hacked into the Forbidden Zone?"

"She opened a temporary window and, with her custom-designed bioscope, she saw through the mask and found a planet inside the Zone. Just as you suspect, Gordy, it was a planet with dynamic atmospheric conditions, markers of oxygenation, the glitter of chlorophyll, and an abundant supply of water."

He was talking about Green Tara. It was bad enough that Gordy was smitten by the legend. Now the Chief was talking about my mother's failed mission, too! I felt dizzy.

"Maureen Bosque had the ability to chart and analyze what others called 'unreadable' information. She was motivated by an intense desire to find a life-supporting planetary home. But, she's gone now." The Chief lowered the wand and the orb evaporated.

Right. Momo was gone now. She'd been gone so long, it hardly mattered any more. But all these reminders made me feel like I was five -years-old again. I clung to the railing, afraid I might fall. Now I had specific information about what Momo intended, and that made her seem real again, like she'd just disappeared.

The Chief handed the navigation wand to Gordy. "Please, put this away." While Gordy carried the wand to its stand at the prow, the Chief spoke quietly but passionately to me. "Perhaps, Virginia, one day you will be motivated by a higher purpose. Perhaps one day you, too, will see what others say is not possible."

Then he left me standing there, gripping the railing.

I heard Dot chime. From the sound, I knew she'd reviewed my test results, and I had passed my qualifying exam. I was one step closer to earning my official pilot's license. But, my personal victory no longer felt so important. What had the Chief meant by a *higher purpose*?

⊕

⊕

Finding Impound

In just a few short hours I'd uncovered more about my mom than I'd *ever* known. The information startled me. Apparently, my mom believed in the legendary planet Green Tara, so much so that she had devised a way to get herself into the Forbidden Zone. The Chief made it sound like she was a genius *and* a hero. I thought it was crazy. Of course, hearing Momo was someone to be admired came with an automatic pride factor. But she'd been reckless to leave me and fly off on an impossible mission, and that made me furious.

I craved privacy, a place I could think. That's what I wanted: the cozy safety of my Blast, which was inconveniently located in Impound. I'd never been to Impound, but this had already become a day of field trip firsts, so why not? Despite my queasiness, I raced out of Navigation and headed toward the aft of the ship.

Gordy followed me. "Where are you going?"

"I want to see where they put my Blast," I said. "You should return to quarters."

He planted himself in between me and an unmarked doorway, blocking my passage.

"What?" I wasn't in any mood to have him tag along.

"I want to show you something, and it's on the way to Impound." He set his fists on his hips and made himself wider. "Besides, you don't even know exactly where to go."

Gordy was right. Impound was beyond the livestock pens in what I guessed would be the stinkiest corner of the ship. But I'd never actually been to the very bottom, below Z-Deck, to double Z. I opened Dot and asked her to bring up the map, so we could find my Blast.

Suddenly, I was so tired I couldn't focus on our coordinates. I was actually relieved when Gordy examined the map, opened the door into the stockyards, and led the way. So much for my plan to get rid of him.

We walked past rows and rows of animal stalls. They all looked the same, but the sounds and odors coming from each shifted radically. As we passed pens—different than the stalls of the four-legged animals—birds frantically hurled themselves against electronic netting. Their singed feathers clouded the air inside their cages, and the acrid smell made my nostrils flare and my eyes water.

I gagged, and for the umpteenth time that day I thought I might vomit.

Gordy tugged my arm and pulled me alongside the first distinctive structure on our route, a greenhouse. It was fairly open, and it was easy to see the orderly rows of planting beds. The plants themselves were not nearly so orderly. They grew in all shapes and sizes. Some of the stalks were straight, but just as many were wildly tangled. And, similar to the projection of vegetation we'd seen in the navigation orb, the plants came in many different colors of green. Some of the leaves were even purple.

Also interesting—though I didn't see anyone—a man was singing a vaguely familiar song. Recorded music was common enough, and I'd seen formal performances, but hearing a single human sing for pleasure was very unusual.

Gordy held up his pocket recorder. "I can add the singing gardener to my a cappella collection."

I thought it was an odd time for Gordy to focus on his music anthropology assignment, but I was happy to take a break where the odors were pleasant. I yawned. Thankfully, the singing was pleasant, too, with a haunting quality, but not in a creepy way.

I sat on a bench where one wild plant spilled out the side of the greenhouse window. It smelled different, brighter than the lavender of Mom's chest of clothes, but it had a similar soothing effect. Dot called it peppermint, and said it could help settle my stomach. It must have, because I no longer felt nauseous just very, very tired. The gardener's song worked like a lullaby and I curled up on the bench. But before I could get any sleep, Gordy put his recorder away and pulled me to my feet.

"Come on, Gin. Rest stop is over."

Past the green house we walked down a slope. Unlike any other deck on ship, the flooring here was not parallel to the ceiling. We definitely walked at an angle for many paces, from Z to ZZ. Where the flooring leveled out and the space narrowed, we came to some synth straw piles, the place where animal waste was sorted into fertilizer and unusable refuse. Zap! All of it was foul.

Worse, we were at a dead end. We were supposed to be at the entrance to the cargo bay, but I didn't see a corridor.

The hair on the back of my neck stood up. That meant a field of static electricity. Then I heard a distinctive whir. I nudged Gordy and pointed to my own eye, our private signal to look out for a SensEye.

He motioned me to a spot between the piles of fertilizer and refuse. Great, now we were stuck hiding in the stinkiest possible location on board ship. If I opened Dot to check the surveillance schedule, the roaming sensor would pick up her presence and ours. So we squatted there silently for what felt like forever, until a magnetically powered SensEye hovered into view.

Gordy waited until the eye was turned away and pulled what looked like a toy pistol out of his boot, aimed and pulled the trigger. I assumed he was playacting. After all, there was no sound or visible evidence that he'd fired anything. But the SensEye wobbled up and down, and its eyelids shuddered.

"What did you do to it?" I whispered.

He held up his little pistol and grinned. "A demagnetizer." He put the pistol back in his boot. "I've been wanting to test it."

"Now they'll just send a secure and repair crew and I'll get sent back to Lockdown."

He shook his head. "It's not broken."

The SensEye had wobbled up the incline, away from us. "It looks broken."

"Its sensors will reset."

"You mean the effect's only temporary?"

He nodded.

Amazing. I had to acknowledge Gordy's victory. "I suppose if they were going to send a crew, we would have heard an alert by now." I opened Dot again and zoomed into a map detail.

"Come on," Gordy said. And he went to the dead end and pulled out some tools from his other boot. "This wall's ..."

". . . an airlock." On the other side there was an outer hull cargo door. I'd figured out the nature of our dead end, too. Obviously, the last bay on ZZ-Deck was where the refuse got dumped *and* where the impound cargo sat. How insulting—my Blast was stored with the ship's trash.

I might have gone to help Gordy spring the airlock, but I heard the strangest squeaking sound. When I looked around the side of a relatively fresh stack of synth straw, the squeaking got louder and more urgent. I saw a pile of tiny, moving balls of fur. "What's this?"

"You found them. That's what I wanted to show you." Gordy laughed and continued to work on the airlock key pad.

Dot said, "Sounds like baby cats, also known as kittens."

I'd heard of kittens, but I had no mental picture of what one looked like.

"Cats are desirable creatures, mammals that keep undesirable mammals, like rodents, in check," she said.

The balls of fur tumbled out of their straw nest. The kittens were all different colors, one orange, one gray, one white, and a black one that crawled up my pant legs and cried. They all sounded so desperate. "What's wrong?"

Dot said, "They're probably hungry and calling for their momma cat."

I peeled the frantic kitten off of my pant leg. It was light, though bigger than the others, and completely black except for a pink nose. I held it close to my body, and it calmed down right away. It was so soft. Different than Dot's plush side, the kitten was warm, and I could feel its breath and another subtle vibration. I knew—not intellectually or based on scientific evidence, but I was absolutely sure— that the kitten felt safe. Something about holding it close to my belly made me feel safe and content, too. Another kitten, a really tiny one, crawled up my back and made it all the way across my tunic and to my shoulder. It was crying. "Dot, if it's hungry, why is it crawling on me? I don't have cat food."

"No, but you are big and warm and more likely to be a food source than the straw," Dot said.

"I'll take that as a compliment." The kitten walked down my arm.

Dot said, "Please don't let her scratch my screen."

I felt the kitten's sharp little claws, and I pulled it off of Dot's plush cover. I set it and the black one down.

"The momma cat will return soon," Dot said. "Unless disaster has befallen her."

"Disaster?" I leaped to the worst. "Like, death?"

"It's more likely that she's trapped somewhere."

"Where do we look?"

"Let your ears be the guide," Dot said. "An adult meow is very similar to a kitten's, but lower in pitch."

I closed my eyes and tried to imagine what an adult cat would sound like. I heard something interesting, but it wasn't a meow. It was a subtle rumble, like the mechanical air exchange, but softer and more rhythmic. I walked around a nearby storage module and saw a larger version of the orange kitten that had clung so tenaciously to my arm. This one was a patchy mix of colors with brown and black spots, too.

"A most whimsical fur pattern, don't you think? The variety of spot sizes is highly variable, yet the look is quite distinctive," Dot said. "It's called a calico."

"Let me file that in a will-never-need-to-be-accessed neural pathway of my brain." I picked up the momma cat, which was considerably heavier than the kittens, but not impossible to carry. I walked back around and, when we got near the nest, momma cat got restless and jumped out of my arms. It was quite a drop for a creature of her small size, but she landed steady and trotted toward the nest. The kittens cried louder than ever, and when she curled around them they nuzzled up to her and instantly fell silent.

I noticed the black kitten was still prancing around. "Dot, why isn't the black one eating with the others?" I aimed Dot's face to get a good view of its constant motion—scooting up the side of the straw, suddenly springing off in a back flip, and landing a full meter away, ten times its body length!

"This one is clearly older than the suckling kittens," Dot said. "Based on size and acrobatic ability, I deduce three to four weeks older."

The black kitten crawled up my pants leg again. The biology of mammals, churning out so many babies sounded so strange and exhausting. "The calico momma had this baby and then a whole nest full of other kittens?"

"Kittens born to one mother at the same time are called a litter," Dot corrected me. "This calico is nursing her litter of kittens, but the black one is a few weeks older, so it was most likely born to another cat."

I lifted it off my pants leg and looked closely at its paws. All it took was a slight touch under its soft toes, and the pointed claws extended slightly. When I released all pressure, one toe at a time, each claw retracted. "So this one's mother is lost, too?"

"Perhaps, she is. But the black kitten may be weaned." Dot explained, "That means it doesn't need to suckle from its mother to get all its nourishment."

"What's this sound it's making?" I detected a funny little rumble, more vibration than sound.

"That is called a purr," Dot said. "When cats are contented, they purr."

I looked at the way the kitten's tail curled one way and then the other, forming a series of question marks. It did look comfortable.

Gordy called from the airlock control pad. "Got it. I'm in the system."

I set the black kitten down and walked back to Gordy's position. "Before you open the airlock, remember to check the air-pressure on the other side."

Gordy laughed, "Yeah, let's not get sucked into deep space."

Dot said, "The air pressure is even, so it's safe to open to the exterior bay."

Gordy nodded and tapped the open command. At first nothing happened, and he shrugged.

Then I heard the distinct sound of pressure release, Pssshhhhhh. The wall parted and opened into a narrow passageway that led into another cavernous room deep in the bowels of the ship.

The black kitten streaked ahead of us, and we walked along rows of various-sized crates and chests, all generic, nothing that was nearly as interesting as our Bosque family chest. Gordy and I rounded a corner and found the kitten stretched out on one of the impound crates as if he'd been there for days. Its tail curled to the right then re-curled to the left. Otherwise it appeared to be completely at rest. Before I realized it was moving again, it pounced onto Gordy's shoulder and without pause launched to another position higher than our heads, disappearing between the stacks.

"That was spooky!" Gordy said.

Just as suddenly, the kitten reappeared ahead of us on the floor and sauntered back, winding its tiny body back and forth against our ankles. Gordy and I both laughed. From a surprise attack to contact that felt like affection—what an interesting creature.

Beyond the last row of cargo, in the back corner of the refuse chamber, we found my red Blast.

The wheels were locked, but that's standard procedure, to prevent pitching and rolling when a ship is docked. I was relieved to see that a harness net held key structural points, too, so even when the exterior door was open to the vacuum of space, my Blast would be secure. My little scramjet looked fine. "Dot, open the hatch."

"The pilot's entrance is on a security patch," Dot said. "If we open it, we'll definitely set off an alert."

Gordy called from the back of the ship, "This one's clear."

I sprinted around where I could see. Technically, this opening was only accessible from the inside. Gordy wiped his magnetic mitt all around the seam. Pshhh. A gentle air pressure release, and the back hatch dropped down.

I couldn't wait to get inside.

⊕

At Last, My Blast

I scrambled past Gordy and stooped low to get inside my Blast.

What a relief. I unrolled Dot on the console, called up my favorite playlist and propped my feet up. I might not be able to fly, but my Blast felt like my own private refuge, the place where I didn't have to please anyone else.

Gordy plopped in the co-pilot's seat and proceeded to test all the adjustment knobs. I knew it was his nature to touch and fiddle with everything, but it was so annoying. My Blast had become . . . crowded. "Gordy! I want to be alone."

He completely ignored me. But I couldn't tell if he was being rude or simply oblivious.

"Please stop," I said between clenched teeth, "before I lose my polite restraint and begin strangling you."

Gordy smiled at me and pulled the kitten out of his tunic. "Come on, Spooky."

I hadn't even noticed when Gordy picked up the little black kitten. And now, apparently, it had a name....Gordy rubbed the kitten's ears between his fingers. Zap. They looked contented.

In one day everything I thought I knew about my mother had gone through a radical revision, and I didn't have a moment to myself to figure it out! Then the kitten jumped from his lap into mine, but this time it didn't feel soft. It felt like a zillion little needles. "Ouch!" I jumped up, and the kitten sprang onto Gordy's head. He looked ridiculous, but instead of laughing I lashed out, "You have to leave now."

Spooky disappeared in a flash. Gordy looked hurt, and I don't think it was from the kitten's claws. He slid out the back hatch.

"Virginia," Dot said, "You know it is not Gordy's curiosity that is getting under your skin."

"Dare say, oh wise one, what is getting under my skin?" I hated when Dot used a stupid old saying to describe my emotional state. I wish she would just say what she meant.

"Virginia, earlier today you read a letter your mother wrote to you ten years ago. It's natural that you're reminded of all the sadness from that time," Dot said. "You're feeling like you have lost her all over again."

The last thing I wanted to think about was sadness and loss. Spooky wrapped his body around my leg and I picked him up. "I've heard your diagnosis of my separation anxiety. Please, don't."

But Dot continued, "I want to reassure you. In many ways you have not lost her. Every time I talk, you are hearing the kinds of words and thoughts that she would use."

This was news, but I didn't want to hear it. I shut Dot off. Instantly, she shot an image out my amber pendant. When Dot overrode voice or touch activation and generated a hologram—a feature she rarely used—I knew it was a big deal. Double big deal this time—the picture she put up in front of me was my mother.

No. No. No. I didn't want to see this. I'd specifically come here to hide from the jumble of Momo memories. Spooky reappeared again, and I held him close to my heart.

"Momo," I whispered, fighting back the tears. I always avoided pictures of her because they made me feel so raw. I said to Dot, "So, you're passing yourself off as a mom clone now?"

"Your mother programmed me, Virginia. Don't you remember?"

"I know that, but ..." I had never, ever, even thought about the source of Dot's personality. I assumed that our way of being with each other had evolved organically. I'd never thought about the programming mind behind Dot and how my mother's voice came through Dot.

Now Dot's hologram of Momo was floating between us. I was there in the moving picture, too. I was a little girl, playing with a toy space ship, a red one, holding it at the end of my outstretched arm and spinning round and round. I tumbled into Momo and we both ended up on the floor giggling. She said, "Ginny, I have one more present. Something special I made just for you. Something that will help you. Even when I'm not here, you can always count on this." She held up a small, fuzzy package for me to open.

While I watched my younger self, I suddenly remembered everything. This was my birthday party, a private one with only Momo and me. She was giving me my presents, and she'd saved the best for last.

From the first touch my special present felt soft. It was so very soft. I pulled the fat ribbon off and buried my face in the plush surface. Over and over, as I touched my nose to each of the big bold polka dots of color, I said, "Dot. Dot. Dot. Dot. Dot. Dot. Dot." Obviously, Dot had gotten her name the very first moment I held her.

Momo unrolled Dot and showed me how her eyes blinked open when I spoke, and she wrapped Dot around my arm like an extra cuff, in the same comfortable position I've been wearing her for years.

Then Momo put the amber pendant around my neck. "There are two parts. Dot's brain is in the amber. You can't see it, but it's there. Always wear this, and she will protect you. She will take care of you and teach you the same way I do." Momo kissed me on the nose.

The hologram evaporated and Momo was gone.

Tears burned my face. I clutched Spooky's warm, purring body to keep from collapsing into a bawling fit. Not long after my fifth birthday Momo left on an exploratory scientific mission. But she never came back. Officially, she was *lost*. Now I wondered if she had given Dot to me just before she left *in case she didn't return*.

I rubbed the smooth, warm amber between my fingers. Yes, Dot had always been with me and protected me. But I missed my Momo. I shut my eyes and remembered how it felt to be curled up in her arms with my face on her neck, safe under the canopy of her ginger scented hair. I had to try and find her. I wanted her back in my life.

Gordy tumbled back into the cockpit. "Gin."

I hated to admit it, but he was right. It was time for a rescue mission. Even if I didn't have enough information, I had to try.

"Do you feel that?" Gordy asked.

At first I thought Gordy meant the feeling I had of longing to see my mother again. In the deepest corners of my body I felt the need to see her in person. For real. To touch and hold.

Then I felt what he was talking about, a strange vibration—not a soothing purr—coming from outside the Blast.

I set Spooky on the dash, and Gordy and I leaned over to look out the window. There wasn't any movement on the floor, just silent rows of cargo. Gordy pointed to the far left corner of the bay. The airlock was closing shut. Psshhhht. I didn't see any sentries or workmen. This outer cargo bay appeared empty, except for the cargo and us. Then the light shifted. Dot said, "Sealing our back hatch." Psshhhht.

Something else was moving outside. We pressed our faces against the window. Sure enough, the exterior bay door, the one in the hull of the ship, started to open.

Good thing we were inside my space-worthy Blast, because that's all that was outside. Deep space.

"Why is the bay door open?" As if reading my mind, Gordy spoke with his most articulate and logical voice. "The only reason to open it would be to unload cargo, or dump refuse, but …"

"… the stinky stuff is still on the other side of the airlock," I continued his thought. "If the refuse that's meant to be swept out of the back side of the ship is on the other side, what kind of cargo is getting unloaded?"

A spherical pod dropped into view. We both looked up. The cargo bay ceiling had opened up and the pod—apparently lowered by a magnetic system, because there was no visible support—spiraled down in front of us.

"It's an exploration pod," Dot said, "Filled with unwilling colonists."

Dot's chilling description, like the pod, came out of nowhere. I was stunned.

The pod was fairly large, six or seven times the size of my two-seater, and it was stuffed with people peering out small windows. I watched the exiles strain against their windows. They waved desperately at us. I'd heard about the practice of dumping colonists whenever the population count rose too high, but I'd never actually seen a pod released into deep space.

"It looks like they're calling for help." I was scared, so to steady myself I went into pilot mode. "Open communications."

Dot said, "It's a Llama 33. The craft only has an automatic transponder. We can't speak to them directly."

"They don't have fully functioning communications?" I wasn't asking Dot a question. I was digesting the cold facts. The colonists didn't have a decent-sized ship with adequate navigation or communication systems. They were being released with virtually no chance of success. It was a death sentence sending them out like that. "We've got to do something," I said.

Gordy nodded, but neither one of us knew what to do. We watched the pod swing closer to the open bay door.

"They've been cut loose," Dot said.

"They need help," I said, feeling more and more helpless.

"I know. But, even if we could fly after them, what then?" Dot said, "Would we improvise a docking maneuver? And then, assuming we could figure out some way to physically connect, what could we do?"

I answered Dot's logical question, "We could only take on one or two." The people inside the Llama 33 stared back at us.

"And then what?" Dot said.

"They'd be considered runaways." I knew that it would be impossible to hide illegals inside the ship for any length of time. SensEyes were everywhere, and Gordy only had one demagnetizer.

"And as soon as the runaways are found?" Dot said.

"They'd be ..." Gordy couldn't finish his sentence.

"The so-called volunteer explorers would be dropped off again." I swallowed hard and considered their likely fate.

Dot said, "Their only chance is to find a favorable system and a place to land."

I held my open hand up hopefully to the pod's crew. One was a girl who looked half my age. Even though I knew their chances were slim, I imagined a planet where the little girl could thrive.

The pod tumbled outside. "Those people … ," Gordy said, choking up.

"Dot, can you transmit the chart to Green Tara?" I just blurted this idea before I even knew it was an idea.

Gordy said, "Yes! You can send the coordinates. I took a snap shot. Here." He put his recorder on top of her screen.

"That's a creative solution." Dot hummed as she packaged the Green Tara star chart and messaged it to the pod.

I didn't say anything, because I didn't want to scare Gordy. But sending the colonists coordinates that might or might not be accurate, to a place that may or may not exist, was not a particularly useful gift. And then there was the problem of their pod's limited navigation abilities. I saw the sun sail open up, so clearly they had power. But that class of pod didn't have any directional controls.

I was physically shaking. Gordy knew most everything I was thinking, so—understatement—this was not a happy moment for either of us. But we'd done everything we could, even if it amounted to nothing for the colonists. Silently, we watched the pod drift farther and farther away from us, until finally the cargo bay door rumbled shut.

Spooky meowed, and I picked him up. At least we'd found my Blast. I sat back in my pilot's seat and I felt the strange vibration again, not the rumble of the bay door, but the comforting little kitten purr.

Soon enough the air pressure would be safe again, and we would be able to leave the cargo hold. But after the shock of seeing the helpless pod released with no way for us to help the people inside, Gordy was still shaking. He looked like he needed the comfort, so I handed Spooky to him.

My mind reeled back to all I'd learned about Momo, and how she'd made birthday gifts to soften the worst possible outcome of her exploratory mission. She'd known the risks. Her search for free air and water was voluntary.

I could get sad again, or I could get angry. I decided to get answers.

My time for a face-to-face with Dad was way overdue.

⊕

⊕

The Family Secret

I really needed to talk to Dad, and I needed to talk to him without Gordy tagging along. Fortunately, Gordy had other things to do. He figured, if his Aunt Maureen could do it, he could hack through the security block, too. So he returned to Navigation to convince the Chief to let him explore whatever parts of the Forbidden Zone he could get into. That left me solo.

I slipped into our quarters through the back door as quietly as possible, because I didn't want to present myself all rumpled and smelly with synth straw stuck to my clothes. My plan was first, take a shower, and second, confront Dad about all his lies.

Sounds harsh, I know. But he'd never, ever mentioned the cruelty of releasing colonist pods. Major information gap. *And* he'd always said Momo was lost. He'd never once let on that he might know where she'd gone or why. That one fell squarely in the category of lies of omission, too.

Zap! I was disappointed.

Angry.

Furious with my dad.

I set Great-gran Vera's manuscript down on the bed and peeled Dot off my arm. I was unsnapping my tunic when I heard the oddest sound. I peered into the main room and saw Dad on his knees trying to repair the cracked display case. But it wasn't what he was doing that sounded odd. It was him. He was weeping.

Instantly, I jettisoned my plan. I'd never seen my dad cry. He never even looked sad or in any way vulnerable. I ran and knelt by his side. "Daddy."

"Virginia." He held me in his giant arms, and I felt safe.

"I'm sorry about breaking the display case," I said.

"No need to apologize." He rocked me gently.

"It was an accident," I said.

"I know. Gordy sent me a message about reversing the gravity controls on your moon boots." Dad brushed the hair from my face. "The eagle feather looks good on you."

I'd forgotten that I'd used the artifact as a hair spike. I pulled it out of my hair and stroked the soft feather, glad there was no apparent damage. "I didn't mean any disrespect."

"It was your mother's most prized possession." He smiled. .

The intricate pattern of veins and barbs fascinated me. No wonder Momo treasured it. I tried to imagine the bird with many, many feathers like the one I held, and felt a kinship with that long-ago creature. The eagle and I both shared a passion for flight.

Dad still held me, and it felt warm and honest.

Wait.

What about the dishonesty surrounding Momo's lost-in-space story?

"Speaking of my mother, when the display case fell over, this shook loose." I pulled Momo's handwritten letter out of my pocket and unfolded it for Dad to read.

His face went white. He let go and stood up, looming over me. Apparently he didn't need to read the whole thing word-for-word to understand the meaning. "She called on you to complete the mission?"

I nodded.

"She can't have you. You're too young."

"What do you mean, she can't have me? I'm too young for what?" Wait. Wait. Wait! We'd been having a tender moment. Sharing and honest. But as soon as I mentioned Momo, Dad locked up. I wasn't going to let him divert me this time. "We've skipped the main part of this story. The part where you lied to me about my mother's disappearance."

This is the moment I thought the vein on the side of his forehead might burst.

Dad gritted his teeth, and said, "I've been protecting you."

"Protecting me from the evils of the legendary planet Green Tara deep inside the big, bad Forbidden Zone?"

"How do you know where she went?" Dad bent down and looked into the now-empty pedestal base. "The chest? You found the manuscript?"

I nodded. "Yes, Dad."

"No one outside the family must ever see it." He sounded nervous and looked around the room. "Is it safe?"

"Gordy has the chest of clothes. The manuscript's in my room. And I'll keep it hidden. But you have to explain one thing to me."

He shifted. "What do you want to know?"

"Explain to me why you never followed Momo. When she got lost, why didn't you rescue her? This time I expect to hear the whole truth."

"It's too much to explain."

"Dad!"

He took a very deep breath and said, "Your mother believed in the legends. That it was …. *is* possible to resurrect Earth and make it so everyone has air and water for free." He sank back down to the floor. "She inherited Vera's manuscript when she was a young girl and studied it very closely. When there was an opening on this colonial cruiser your mother was the first to sign on. I was with her then. We got married so we would get the same assignment. I loved her, of course, and we had a shared vision. We knew the cruiser's flight path would eventually take us near Green Tara. This was my mission, too."

Part of the story I recognized. Dad always said he took his job on the colonial cruiser to follow Momo. But he'd never spoken to me about their secret destination.

"We thought it would take 25 years to travel far enough," Dad said. "But the cruise ship's course changed unexpectedly. You were still a little girl. Only five. When we came near enough to Tara, your mother insisted . . . You have to understand, Maureen and I were partners. The full scope of my commitment was to both her and to the Earth Restoration Alliance. But we had a commitment to you, too. We couldn't both go."

"So you let her go alone?"

"It was your mother's birthright, as Vera's granddaughter. Plus her research with her bioscope allowed for flexible off-deck flights. So, she had the opportunity." Tears ran down his cheeks. "She was only supposed to be gone for a few days. Fly to Tara, collect the plant specimens, transport them to Earth—if, and only if, she could find and operate the hyperspace jump point—and return to ship."

I'd asked for the whole story, but Dad's explanation was sketchy. Momo planned to harvest specimens, transport them to Earth, and be back in a few days? I thought hyperspace was just a theory. I wanted my mother to have a solid, realistic plan, one that she could survive.

Dad was still weeping. "She was supposed to return. Any part of the mission she couldn't complete solo, we would solve together and try again. And again. As many times as necessary. " He stood up and paced around the room. "Obviously, something went wrong. Celia, your Aunt Celia, intercepted a security message about a Forbidden Zone violation."

I nodded, "No flights are allowed to cross into the Zone."

"I scrambled her ship's locators, so she wasn't tracked into the Zone. But I must have missed something." Dad stopped in front of me, head bowed. His voice and eyes took on a pleading look, like he wanted me to forgive his mistake. This was a huge admission, because my dad never makes mistakes. "Your mother's research mission, launched as a fully authorized bioscope flight, triggered an investigation. Celia jumped ship impulsively, without any prior communication with me, and she flew to warn Maureen." His strained voice choked. "Then they were both lost."

I could see and hear how sad he was. "So, Aunt Celia went after my mother to find her?"

"She flew into the Forbidden Zone, but changed course and went in another direction." Dad started pacing again. "She wanted to create a diversion that would lead security patrols away from Tara. That's been my guess, but it's only a guess. Neither one of them have been heard from since. Their disappearance reinforced the Triumvirate's safety rationale for blocking any more exploration within the Zone."

I said, "You knew where they were when they disappeared, and you didn't do anything to help them?"

"I couldn't. I . . . It's complicated. Someone had to take care of you, Virginia, and the baby. Gordy was so little. He was barely walking. I couldn't leave you both here alone. Your mother made me promise."

"I'm not a baby any more. Let's go now. We can find her now."

"It's not that simple. We can't just jump ship without a flight plan. The Triumvirate won't relinquish control." He sighed. "The political climate isn't right."

"I've heard you say those exact words a trillion times."

"Oh, Virginia." He sounded tired. "There's more to it. We will find the right time, and we will go find her."

I hated Dad in his default control mode. "The time will never be right for you. You've just given up."

He stroked my head. "Your mother never gave up. And you have her same great spirit." Dad bent down, kissed me on my cheek, and whispered, "I miss her, too."

I felt comforted by the safety of his touch, by the glimmer of what my mother was like and that Dad saw *her same great spirit* in me.

Suddenly, he wiped his face and stood up, a signal he was back-to-business, and something inside me collapsed. I felt hollow.

"I saw that you passed your final star chart test. Congratulations, sweetheart." Dad said, patting my back. "Someday I know those skills will be put to good use."

Dad was already pulling away, detached, straightening his collar. I knew he was just trying to defuse my energy.

But before I could mount another plea for action, a com disc in his pocket lit up. It was urgent, bright orange, and meant he was called to his post. He glanced at the message and muttered, "Interesting." Then, as if our previous conversation—the profound and meaningful revelations about Momo and her grand mission to Green Tara—had never happened, he picked up the pieces of the fallen display case and carried them out of our quarters.

"Love you," he said, as he left me sitting alone on the floor.

Wait a blazing bolide. Momo had been stranded for a decade. Dad actually knew where she'd gone. *And* he was in zero rush to figure out how to rescue her. Was I supposed to figure this out all by myself?

⊕

⊕

Convincing Evidence

I sprawled on my bed. Now it was my turn to weep. Zap. Crying made my sinus cavities ache, and I felt hot. My tears were hot. Even my chest was hot. I looked down, and saw my amber pendant glowing white. No wonder I was feeling the heat. Dot was turning up the thermostat.

A light shot out of the amber, like a genie from a bottle. This time the hologram Dot made was her face. She floated above me, her eyes chiseled like stone and her eyebrows bristling. On her screen all she ever showed was her eyes. But her 3-D face included a very wide mouth. In a deep, booming voice she said, "Quit wallowing."

"I'm grieving, Dottie."

"Save it for later. We've got work to do. Look at the amber. Really look." As soon as she was done giving orders, Dot's hologram flowed back in the pendant.

I held up the warm amber and wiped away my tears. The surface was smooth, but the amber wasn't perfectly clear. It had flaws, natural to the organic fossil. I rolled over and reached for Dot's flex form. "Show me a detail view." I laid the amber pendant on top of Dot's smooth side. Once magnified, I could see the corners of her brain, the gold processor, embedded in the golden amber. But all around the chip, what to the naked eye were blurry spots in the stone, now looked like strands of floating seaweed.

"I don't remember ever looking so closely at your brain," I said. "Magnify by another factor of ten."

Dot zoomed into a microscopic view and close-up the seaweed looked like multi-colored wheels. "Dottie, this looks like single-cell organisms."

She said, "Yes, my brain is permeated with an organism that is currently in stasis. In other words ..."

"I know what stasis means. But what is it?" I asked.

"Look in the manuscript under *phytoplankton*."

I flipped to a page in the center of Great-gran Vera's book. The painted picture looked just like the microscopic algae floating deep inside my amber pendant. "It's a plant."

"An aquatic plant. Notice there's more than one kind. Look at all the varieties."

I turned page after page and looked at dozens of magical shapes, all labeled phytoplankton. "Do you think this is important?"

Dot didn't say a word, but her steely eyes said *this is most important*.

I read the description and said, "The basic idea is phytoplankton is filled with enzymes and chlorophyll, and in a natural environment—not when it's in stasis laced in with your brain—it functions as a major oxygen generator."

The iris of Dot's eyes took on the geometric pattern of one of the phytoplankton.

"Don't go seaweed on me," I said.

Dot chortled and her eyes morphed into a pair of fish that darted away.

I was left with Great-gran Vera's hand-made encyclopedia, information about Momo's mission to Green Tara, and Dot's emphatic lesson about phytoplankton. It was up to me to tie together the different threads. I reread Momo's letter and poured over Great-gran Vera's manuscript, especially the entries on the microscopic algae of the sea.

While I read, Dot played music—that's our normal way of working—something new downloaded from Gordy's recorder. I recognized it as the man's voice we'd heard coming from the greenhouse. This time I listened closely to the lyrics.

"Old amber sparks and melts the juice.
The deep sea breathes.
Life blooms in salty water,
Cool, clear water.

It's time to sing for Mother Earth.
The deep sea breathes.
Each star's a pool of water,
Cool, clear water."

The singer's voice was far from perfect, and when he went to the higher notes it grew raspy. But the rough texture was filled with something indefinable, wrapping around the smooth words, adding resonance to *bloom* and *cool*.

I didn't know exactly what the song meant, but I loved the last part, "Each star's a pool of water, cool, clear water." Dot and I both sang along when the greenhouse gardener repeated those lines.

I shut my eyes and let the sound of the gardener's voice wash over me—*cool, clear water…* I could have drifted peacefully to sleep. I was tempted. But there was so much going on. I said, "Time for a log entry—

Dot log: 244 years ACE, 3 months, 17 days

Dear Dot,

The evidence has become impossible to ignore. We have a handwritten letter from my mother, the Chief says she opened a window to the Forbidden Zone and saw a life-supporting planet, and even Dad—withholder of all truly important facts—admitted he believed in the legend of Green Tara. More than simply believing in a planet with a viable biosphere, he confirmed that it was my mother's last known destination."

I sat up. "Dottie, let's look at the manuscript again. Maybe we'll find more clues." I flipped through Greatgran Vera's book until I found a page of planetary maps.

"That looks promising," Dot said with a deep, clipped, possibly Egyptian accent. "It's quite possibly the information we would need on an expedition across the wilderness." Her eyes melted into a quivering image. It looked familiar and when the mirage sharpened, I recognized the scene from my favorite 20th century movie from old Earth. Three men on horseback, an archeologist, his scholarly father, and their friend and guide, traveled through the Canyon of the Crescent moon on a quest for the Holy Grail.

"Dot, please scan whatever you think might be useful." She responded with the theme music from *The Last Crusade*.

I unwrapped her and rolled her face down onto the book. She glowed, and I curled up next to her.

Obviously, I needed a plan. Momo had left us the star chart. But how would I get my Blast out of impound and into the Forbidden Zone?

⊕

⊕

Preparing for the Mission

Two days later, the night steward was frantically sorting food trays on a delivery cart in the main galley and muttering something about a banquet on A-Deck. On more than one occasion I'd gotten access to locations simply by offering to carry food to the crew. This time, my whole plan hinged on delivering food to the late shift. I tapped his shoulder. "I'll take the supper tray to navigation. I'm headed down."

He wiped sweat from his bald head. "Delivery isn't a proper job for a young scientist-in-training. But ... " Just as I anticipated, the steward spun the cart around, pulled out a tray, and handed it to me. "Virginia, you're a shooting star. Take it away."

Zingo.

I left the galley through the swinging doors and stopped in the staff dining hall, where I accidentally flicked a little food into the SensEye at the condiment counter. Oops. Before it had time to clear its view, I slipped a small capsule from my sleeve, cracked it open, and sprinkled fine, white grains over the hot food. It was just a standard sedative in a larger than average dose. Not enough to harm anyone, but plenty extra to make sure it worked quickly.

Then I left the mid-ship dining hall and zapped down to Z-Deck.

The tube stopped at navigation, and when the door opened Gordy met me. "Success?" Gordy really could be great. It had been his idea to grind the sedative capsules and hide it in the supper. Too bad I'd have to ditch him before I jumped ship.

I handed the food tray to him. "Just a little something to relax the crew."

He smiled and took the tray to the navigator on duty for the night shift, the only crewman in the bay.

It was Ray.

If I'd known, I would have picked another time, because I didn't like the idea of tricking Ray. Not again.

He waved to me.

I pretended I didn't notice and walked the other way—close enough to listen in, but not close enough to be part of his supper conversation. I'd just assumed it would be someone I didn't know. Feeding a generic crewman the sleeping powder without his knowledge wouldn't have felt so personal.

While Ray ate, I studied historical star charts on the other side of the bay. No one else was in the bay, so I looked for more evidence of the Tara system. Even though the Forbidden Zone was wiped from the official records, a careful look at the nearby systems showed gravitational forces at work. Interesting.

When Ray was done, he said, "Thanks for the food service." Gordy cleared his tray. "Something tells me you're not here to earn marks toward a steward's post."

Did he suspect we were planning something outside normal navigation protocol?

"I like it here when . . ." Gordy jumped in, sounding perfectly innocent, and then paused mid-sentence.

" . . . when it's quiet," Ray completed the thought. "Me, too. And here, we have access to the best toys on board. Want to look at our current position?"

"Always." Gordy leapt to the navigation orb.

Ray ambled to the orb and opened the current star chart. "Today the Chief showed me the technique for following the flight path. Do you know how?" Gordy nodded, and Ray handed the navigation wand to Gordy. "Good. Show me where we're going." He settled back in the cushioned command chair and yawned.

Gordy used the wand to maneuver the star chart forward and aft. The Forbidden Zone was obvious, all along the stern of our cruise ship's flight path. Ray yawned again and his eyes drooped shut. The sedative was already taking effect.

I closed the historical charts and, careful not to disturb the dozing apprentice navigator, crept over to the central orb. From a different angle I peered into the thick orange haze. Not that I actually expected to see anything new, but I was curious. And as I leaned over the curved railing, my pendant swung free of my tunic.

"You always wear that." Ray startled me. He was smiling sleepily and pointing to my pendant.

I leaned the other way and whispered to Gordy, "Did he eat it all?"

Gordy nodded and shrugged.

I stepped toward the command chair, holding the amber. "It's very old, supposedly from the mythical planet Green Tara." I took it off and held the hypnotic amber up to the light. "Would you like to see?"

Ray reached out to touch the amber. "Odd."

"If you look closely, it looks like the fossilized plant is still growing." Slowly, I swung the pendant closer and dropped it into his open palm.

He smiled. "Perhaps it's a piece of Green Tara trapped in the amber." Then, as if the weight of his arm grew beyond his strength, he dropped his arm and yawned. "I think it's fascinating that you own a piece of a legend."

If he hadn't sounded so sleepy, I might have left the bay to avoid more conversation. But I continued in bedtime story mode. "Silly, though. How could an object come from a place that never existed?"

"Maybe it did exist. Maybe it does exist. It should. The legend of Green Tara keeps hope alive." He drifted off. "Lovely Tara. The promised land of ancestral songs. The home of our dreams." His eyelids fluttered closed again.

I motioned for Gordy to stay quiet, tiptoed around Ray's side, and took my amber pendant from his relaxed fingers. His breathing grew deeper. I leaned his command chair back as far as it would go. He still didn't stir, and I felt confident he was sound asleep.

I stepped up to the console next to Gordy. "Did you get in?"

"Yes, but ..."

I ignored the *but* and fit the edge of my amber pendant into a drive slot. I opened the corner to Dot's face and whispered to her, "When you're ready."

Dot hummed and her processor, embedded in the pendant, took control of the ship's navigation system. The amber glowed while her main brain worked, and on the console a name registered. It read, *Green Tara.*

At the orb the orange haze dissolved and a planet inside the Forbidden Zone lit up. I'd seen plenty of star systems and planets on display, but seeing this one was different. This planet had been my mother's last known destination.

My throat tightened. I croaked, "Get us closer."

Now that we had confirmation of Momo's coordinates, my goal was to get the cruise ship close enough that I could fly the Blast the rest of the way.

Dot glowed and hummed. "No can do," she said. "Official Triumvirate craft are hard-wired to prevent even accidental drift into the Zone."

Suddenly, the lights throughout navigation dimmed. Dot scowled. "There's been a security disruption. And I don't mean by us."

It only lasted a moment. Then the lights came back up full. I pressed Dot to find a way around the Zone navigation boundaries. "Use Dad's pass."

"That's the first one I tried," Dot said.

"The Chief's?" suggested Gordy.

"Access denied," Dot said.

An alarm sounded. Alternating blue and orange lights flashed on the far end of the console.

"Breach alert on C-Deck, the port side," Dot said.

"It's probably a little meteor hit. Not our problem," I said, even though any kind of meteor was a serious situation. I simply couldn't allow any distraction.

Gordy looked at the message closely and said, "We've been boarded, Gin. By unauthorized personnel."

"Who boarded the ship?"

"It doesn't say who. Just that it's an unauthorized boarding by an undetermined number of people."

Great. The authorization protocols were so tight that anybody could set off security alarms, but now the ship would be on increased alert for renegades and outlaws. "Tranquillo. This isn't the first place patrols will come if an alarm originates on C-Deck."

"But if the second mate doesn't answer, they'll send a patrol to check the room," Gordy said, reminding me of the security breach—imagined or real—procedures.

We both looked at Ray. He was snoring softly.

"We don't want to get him in trouble. And we don't want to deal with a security patrol," I said.

"Right," Gordy said. "I'll send an *all clear* response from navigation."

While Gordy played around with the alarm, I studied the navigation orb.

"If we can't get the cruise ship into the zone, we need to trick the system into moving the Forbidden Zone boundary to the far side of Green Tara." I was frustrated I didn't know how to do what I wanted. Nothing I did with the navigational wand had any effect.

Gordy succeeded in turning off the flashing alert lights. He grabbed the wand from me and plugged in a Triumvirate override code. "I've been saving this one for when we really needed it." The Forbidden Zone boundary floated starboard of our flight path, leaving Green Tara in the clear.

"Sweet," I said.

Dot said, "Setting course to the outer rings of the Tara system."

"Remember, Dottie, before you unplug, load the Zone disguise sequence."

"Zone disguise sequence?" Gordy asked.

"Navigational memory won't show tonight's record of what we're doing and where we're going. Tomorrow, even the Chief Navigator won't know that the Forbidden Zone space was temporarily adjusted, much less violated."

"Double sweet," Gordy said.

"Let's jet!" I replaced the amber fossil around my neck and closed Dot at the cuff. "Gordy, you know where my Galaxy Blast is."

"It's the only red scramjet in impound."

"I need you to get it ready to take off from the cargo deck." I knew he would understand what I had in mind, and he seemed delighted with his assignment. While he zipped to cargo, I planned to return to the Bosque quarters and retrieve Great-gran Vera's manuscript. It had been the source of all the decisive clues so far. I felt sure it would be the essential guidebook for my mission.

I stepped into a rarely used transport tube and stole one last look at Ray. Even though he was smiling peacefully, I felt a little guilty about knocking him out. But the less he knew, the better. I wouldn't want him to face another ugly interrogation.

⊕

⊕

The Pirate Twins

The breach alert flashed in every transport tube and corridor, but I managed to slip up to K-Deck without seeing anyone. Good. Just around the bend from our family quarters I heard giggling. Not good. I stopped and whispered into Dot's cuff, "Take a sneak peek." Then I pulled my personal SensEye out of my pants pocket and rolled the small sphere down the corridor. It stopped just past the corner. Perfect placement.

Dot whispered, "Looks like a pair of pirates."

Pirates? That term belonged to an era when ships sailed the seven seas of Earth. If the situation had been less tense, I probably would have laughed. I peeled open Dot's face to get a look at the picture. It was just a pair of redheaded teenage girls. Why was she calling them pirates? I presumed these were some of the unauthorized personnel, listed in the security alert.

I whispered, "They look my age." They also looked very much alike. The only things that set them apart were their hairstyles and the patterns of their blouses and pants.

Dot did a quick database search and compared her live picture with one from her files. After adjusting the file image for age, Dot confirmed, "Looks like the twins: Lora and Lee." Labels at the bottom of each picture identified Lora, the twin with a short bob, and Lee, who wore her red hair in a ponytail.

Neither looked dangerous. "These two hacked through the cruiser security?"

"You and Gordy just hacked through cruiser security."

"Your point?"

"Cruiser security is vulnerable. Also, I doubt they're alone. These girls may not appear to be threatening, but they are members of a larger group, the Skats."

"Skats? That's a strange name." I was pretty sure *scat* meant animal excrement.

"The Skats' original hideout was found by following the right ascension and declination from Sol to Skat, the third brightest star of the Constellation Aquarius."

"Aquarius, the water bearer. Aren't they a little far from home?"

"Apparently, these pirates like to travel." Dot's eyes shifted suddenly.

I heard the girls approaching. I folded Dot's face down so that nothing showed but her polka-dotted cover, and she looked like a simple decorative sleeve. I thought it best to keep Dot under wraps.

The twins rounded the bend and saw me. Lora, the girl with the short bob, glanced at the small SensEye on the floor and pocketed it. Lee, the one with the ponytail, intercepted me. "Wait a minute, girlee." She spun me around, and my amber pendant swirled outward.

Lora grabbed it in mid-air. "Lookee what we got here." She pulled it over my head.

I protested, "Hey. That was my mother's."

"Oh, well. It's my mother's now." Lee giggled.

"It's not even valuable," I said. "It's just a keepsake."

"What's it made of?" Lee asked.

"Looks like amber," Lora said.

"That's worth something," Lee said.

I stepped between them. "But it's not true amber. Look," I pointed to the algae embedded in the fossil and lied, "It's a manufactured fake. And it's tainted."

"A bit murky." Lee nodded.

"But still, worth something." Lora giggled.

I said, "I've got something better." The twins paused. "Return my pendant, and I'll give you something really valuable."

They both eyed me for a moment, then looked at each other. Lora raised an eyebrow, and Lee smiled.

Lora and Lee followed me into my quarters, and I showed them the eagle feather. While the twins tickled each other, I backed up into my sleeping chamber and slid Great-gran Vera's manuscript under my bed so the Skats wouldn't see it.

Lee waved the feather in the air like a question mark. "What's it worth?"

"It's the only one in the galaxy. That makes it priceless." I carried my small jewelry box like an offering.

"Priceless? What's this?" Lee opened the jewelry box lid and ogled the trinkets inside. "Girlee, I like you."

"Ditto! Lee, we could take her with us!" Lora said.

"Perry said: no more kidnaps. Causes too much trouble with the Triverts." Lee made an obscene gesture. Lora mirrored her sister.

I didn't know who Perry was, but I was glad he was anti-kidnapping. I understood 'Triverts' to mean all things associated with the Triumvirate Corporation. "How do you avoid the Triumvirate Law?" I whispered, drawn to the way they flaunted defiance.

"We've got a way," Lora said.

"In the Forbidden Zone," Lee said.

"Danger," Lora said.

"Keep out," Lee said.

Lora whispered, "'Cept it's not a wasteland."

Lee whispered, "It's teeming with life."

"Look at us." Lora pranced in a circle.

"We're way too wild for Triverts." Lee grinned and stuck the eagle feather in my hair. "The feather's way too soft for loot."

Lora returned my amber pendant and accepted the jewelry box as a fair exchange. "Good girl."

The twins laced their arms with mine and swung me around in a light-hearted dance. It was a simple two-step that everyone knows, but they caught me off guard and I stumbled. They just laughed and swung me around again, the second time slow enough for me to match their steps. I played along, to keep them happy with me and the whole exchange. And it seemed to work. They left my quarters singing a tune with an odd, compelling rhythm.

After a quick shower, I put on my pants and tunic, wrapped Dot around my arm in transport mode, and added an extra layer of planetary expedition clothes, a green jacket with multiple pockets and a pair of high boots. Finally, I loaded Great-gran Vera's illuminated manuscript into a back sling.

Just as I was getting ready to leave our quarters, Dad called over the com-line. "Ginny, the ship's been infiltrated by a band of outlaws."

"By pirates," I said, "By the Skats."

"What? How do you know their name?"

"It's derived from a star that defines the territory of their original hideout."

"You be careful. Those characters are unpredictable," Dad said.

"They like me."

"What do you mean, they like you?"

"I met a couple of the girls in the corridor," I said. "At first they were a little intimidating, but honestly, Dad, if they weren't pirates, I think we'd be friends."

"They are pirates, and they are *not* safe," he said. "Stay inside and lock yourself in. Do not, under any circumstances, get involved with them."

"You take care of yourself, Dad. I have a feeling they won't respond as kindly to you. The authority figure thing doesn't go over with them."

"Virginia! Did you hear what I said about staying in your room?"

"I'm fine. Really. Bye, Dad." The 'bye' rolled off easily. Even though somewhere in the deepest corner of my brain I must have realized I was saying goodbye for an extended period of time.

And I could get lost like my mother.

If I really thought about what I was doing, I would have gotten scared or sentimental or responded to Dad's orders.

So I didn't think. I simply acted on what I had to do. When I heard Dad pleading, "Virginia!" I closed the com-line. This time, I couldn't obey dad. This time I was motivated by what Momo had said. Now, it was up to me. She'd had faith in me, even when I was only a little girl.

I tucked the amber necklace inside my tunic, and stepped out of our cabin.

⊕

Return to Impound

Though I didn't follow Dad's orders about staying inside our quarters, everyone else seemed to be observing the high-security alert. The corridors were practically deserted. If the current alarm was accurate, the number of "unauthorized personnel" onboard was thirteen. Based on my encounter with the twins, I didn't believe I was risking my life if I were to run into any of the other Skats, but I still took precautions and avoided the main transport tubes. Instead, I climbed in the dumbwaiter, a small tube designed for packages, curled up in a squat position and zapped down to double Z, to the place beyond the greenhouse near the cargo bay where my Blast sat in impound.

The synth straw next to the air lock looked the same as I remembered, but was not nearly as stinky as it had been when Gordy and I had first found the Blast. I peered into the airlock window. Where was he?

"Hide, Gin." Gordy reached out of the straw and tugged the back of my pant leg.

"Hey, lighten up," I said.

"Not safe," Gordy said.

"Safe from what?" A flash of brilliant color filled the narrow space.

Gordy grabbed my arm and pulled me under cover. He whispered, "Shhhhh. Pirates."

I followed Gordy's look, and knew at a glance that the pack of characters descending on ZZ-Deck were outlaws. There was nothing sedate or discreet about them. They wore flashing shirts laced with conductive wiring. They all swaggered as they walked, and every few steps were punctuated with a weird honking sound. When one of the pack saw a SensEye following him, he covered the eye with his hat and another smacked it down with a flat bat. No doubt, these fellows were from the same clan as the twins. I whispered, "Skats. And they're not afraid of the Triumvirate."

They were carrying a pair of plump birds with long necks and rounded beaks, apparently the source of the honking sound. Then one of them, the tallest and scrawniest of the lot, found the nest of kittens and stuck a white one under his shirt. He sniggered, "I've got my own piece of fur, that's what I've got."

Gordy lurched as if to save the kittens. But I held him back.

They all laughed heartily, including a barrel-chested man. He said, "Tickled pink, eh?" The one with the kitten nodded with a goofy grin. "Warming your heart, eh?" The big man jabbed a knuckle ring under the scrawny man's chin, "It's not food and it's not worth a coin. Now put it back."

"Easy off, Perry." The skinny man dropped the white ball of fur into the straw. I was surprised how gently he handled the little kitten.

Perry, apparently the leader of the pack, said, "No reason to stay in the bottom of the barrel. The upper crust has the loot worth looting." The others agreed with a variety of grunts and headed toward the transit tube.

Once the outlaws whisked away to upper decks, Gordy and I rolled out of the straw. He triggered the opening sequence to the triple air-lock door again. Pssssht. And we entered the cargo bay.

Gordy waved from the backside of the red space coupe. "Everything's ready for takeoff."

"I take it— no real problem?" I said.

"Not for the master," Gordy said, strutting a bit. "I've already secured all the hatches."

"Excellent work." I hopped onto a wing and into the open cockpit.

Gordy followed me up, and Spooky followed him. They both watched while I spread Dot out on the console, and she initiated the pre-flight checklist.

Dot said, "I've already turned off the transponder, and because this Blast is a one-of-its-kind prototype that never went through official manufacturing, we have no locator chips embedded in the systems."

Gordy sat in the co-pilot's seat. "They won't be able to track us."

"Won't be able to track me." I buckled into the pilot's seat and waved good-bye to Gordy.

But, he didn't budge, saying, "This is a mission for two."

"Oh, no, Gordy. You're too young."

"You sound like your Dad." That made it easy for me to push the eject button.

Gordy popped out of the cockpit and landed in a stack of used straw.

I shouted down to him, "I've got Dottie. She won't let me get lost."

"No, Gin. *We're* not getting lost *together*. I'm coming with you." Gordy stood up. He could barely see over the wing into the Blast, but he looked determined. Spooky skittered up his left side, and Gordy clung to the kitten.

"Gordy, the best way you can help me find Momo is to mask my departure. Just in case someone's watching." He had that unmistakable expression on his face, *Don't leave me.* But I was even more determined than him. To sweeten my orders, I added, "Please."

He scowled, but he did back up while I maneuvered the scramjet out of its parked position.

"Once you're safe back inside the air lock, jettison the straw," I said. "I'll use it to cover my escape."

"It'll take me a few minutes to reprogram the cargo bay door," Gordy grumbled as he walked around the backside of my red two-seater.

"Thanks!" I'd easily tossed off my good-bye to Dad, but this time the bye stuck in my throat. I hesitated. Could I really pull off this rescue mission on my own? I always complained about Gordy tagging along with me everywhere, but I was used to it.

Finally I said, "Wish me luck," but I didn't get much volume behind it. Gordy couldn't have heard me.

I closed the cockpit and pointed the Blast's nose toward the outer hull door.

I waited for what seemed like forever—probably only a few minutes—until I felt the distinctive vibration. The cargo bay door parted. I was facing deep space. Used straw and refuse spewed out in front of me, temporarily ruining my star view, but providing the perfect camouflage for my departure. This was it.

"Ready, Dot?"

"All systems are online," she said.

"Release the gravity lock."

Psshhhhhht.

Disconnect.

I didn't feel anything strapped securely in my pilot's seat, but I could see the cargo bay drop behind us as we tumbled silently amidst the straw and refuse. My serene cockpit shell held tight, in stark contrast to the random stuff without direction or form floating outside my little Blast. As we drifted further and further away from the cruise ship and deeper into the Forbidden Zone, my thoughts raced in a jumble. I felt thrilled to be on my own, on the most important mission of my life. I was also painfully alone in the vast distance between stars.

⊕

Escape

I watched the Colonial cruiser pull away, headed back to its original flight path. The mammoth ship had locked into the flight-path disguise instructions Dot and I had programmed into its navigation. Meanwhile, in my Blast, we were still floating freely so we would remain undetected by the Triumvirate security scanners.

"Our strategy's working, Dot!" The Blast rotated slowly until we could no longer see the pot-bellied eyesore.

Dot hummed, open and relaxed, spread out on the console where she was peacefully monitoring our position in space.

I stroked her soft edge. "Show me the Green Tara system."

She highlighted a spot in the upper port corner of our window, and there was the unmistakable glow of a nearby star system. A distant star would look like a single point of light. This was a blurrier, larger egg shape with the bright star, the system's sun, in the center. The glow came from the reflected light, bouncing off of planets, moons, asteroids, and smaller solid particles, all held together by the gravitational pull of the Tara sun.

The Blast continued to turn freely, and we lost our view of our destination. All I could see were the stars of deep space, our galaxy. This was my favorite view, and so familiar, so comforting. I took a deep breath, letting all the excitement of my escape drain from my body. I closed my eyes. I was tired.

Then, the enormity of my actions hit me.

I'd never been so alone before.

"Virginia," Dot said, gently.

I opened my eyes to the distant star view.

On the window Dot drew a box around a dark area. "This is the cruise ship's position." It was far enough away that it was no longer visible.

"We have the distance we need?" I asked.

"Yes."

I adjusted the wing and tail flaps to pull the Blast around and, once the Tara system was back in our line of site, I opened the convertible top, exposing the ion engine above the cockpit.

"Let's jet." I pressed the power button, instantly putting more distance between Triumvirate control and us.

The Blast was a smooth ride and we weren't fighting any gravitational force. What I felt was the unmistakable rush of freedom.

"You are piloting like a pro," Dot said. Her translucent face glowed, and she made the oddest, giddy sound, like she was super-charged from our great escape, too.

The cruise ship had brought us close to our destination, and in no time we slipped into the outer cloud of the Green Tara system.

"Can't see much through the ice chips." Dot spoke in a Cockney dialect. "Let's take a closer look, my lady."

I knew she was having fun when she played with character voices. I pulled a telescopic viewer from the side storage pocket and fit the lens to my eye. Before I'd only been focused on the star system as a single destination. For the first time I looked at the planetary objects in detail. "It looks crowded." At a quick glance it looked like two-dozen planets on three different orbital planes.

Dot said, "Magnifying for my lady."

My view shifted. One of the planets, the seventh from the star, the one glowing like an emerald, filled the eyepiece. "Green Tara," I whispered, "Oh, Dot, I never thought a planet could be so beautiful."

"Yes, my lady. It is indeed."

Dot's new character was a radical departure from her normal routines. "Where did *My Lady* come from?"

Dot's face took on the quality of sheet music and she played harpsichord from 18th century Earth. "I was intrigued by the dialog of the stage play you studied in your last comparative literature assignment, and in particular the way the chamber maid spoke to her maiden, My Lady," Dot giggled, like a chamber maid.

I felt giddy, too. There was something fitting about her choice of character and music from an ancient colonial era. We were on a grand adventure and a sense of romance was in the air.

In a completely different character voice, Dot sounded a gruff warning. "Pirates! My Lady. Pirates!"

I laughed, assuming Dot was reciting dialog from another play.

Dot stayed in character voice, but the words were her own. "Ship o' the Skats. To the port side. Closing in."

I scanned the nearby space and saw the outlaw ship headed straight toward us. "Why are you talking like a make-believe character?" We had to hide, but the ice chips at the edge of the Tara system were too small to hide behind. I spotted a nearby plasma cloud. Its natural magnetic charge might work to conceal us. "Let's jet!" Even before she answered, I aimed toward the plasma.

"Temperature, wind speed, radiation levels—all within our tolerance," she said, finally resetting her voice to normal.

I zigzagged into the plume. I had a plan. If we matched the electromagnetic charge of the plasma around us, the tiny Blast would be almost impossible to detect. "Dot, collect some negative ion exhaust on the surface of our ship."

While Dot whirred into action, I slowed the Blast to a hover. The exterior hull of the Blast sparkled with Dot's static charge.

Within moments the outlaws' ship slowed. It circled near our position, but not around us. "It worked. They don't know exactly where we are," I said.

"True. But in their confusion they might bump into us."

"We need to avoid direct contact. Any ideas?"

"I've built up a significant static charge on the hull of the Blast," Dot said.

"I don't want to repel them. They'd just come back. I want to direct their attention away from us."

"Shall I throw a bolt?"

"Brilliant idea. But don't hit them. Just scare them." I opened the electron beam and pointed it in the general direction of our pursuers. "Now!"

The static charge on the hull of the little Blast rippled and threw a bolt. The larger ship froze.

"Let's make it look like a brewing storm," I said.

"Throw another bolt, My Lady?"

"Dot, cut the comedy. Focus."

"Unfortunately, in hover mode we don't burn through many electrons. It will take some time to collect another charge."

"They've started a scan." I watched a console monitor. "It's coming round."

"Five, four, three, two and CHARGE!" Dot shot another bolt in the direction of the Skats' ship.

"Zap!"

"Beware, My Lady."

"Would you quit calling me that?" I could see the other ship was still scanning.

"Preparing another bolt," Dot said. The cabin lights dimmed and all the internal machinery went quiet while Dot built up another charge.

"Meow."

I couldn't believe Dot was playing another character, teasing me again in this moment of crisis.

"That's a distinctly feline sound," Dot said. Apparently, she wasn't the one who meowed.

I got up and dug around in the confined space coupe. I saw a small black tail. "Dot, I found a stow away" I lifted Spooky out from behind the life support bin and returned to my chair holding the kitten.

Then I heard a sneeze. I spun around and saw more movement from the storage bin. Up popped – "Gordy!"

"It's a little tight in here," he said.

"I don't believe you! We agreed you'd stay and deflect attention away from my departure," I said.

"That's what you wanted. I never agreed," he said.

"No wonder the Skats came after me," I said.

"Us. They're after us," he said.

Dot interrupted. "Buckle up. The Skat scan's coming round again."

Gordy made himself at home in the co-pilot's seat. "Love the way you outsmarted them, Gin."

"Stop flattering me," I said.

"Five, four, three, two, CHARGE!" Dot threw another bolt of lightning. To avoid the shock, the Skat ship spun away.

Gordy and I held our breath. Spooky stopped purring. We all watched the Skat ship reel out of control.

When it finally stabilized, the ship sliced a hole in space, flashed inside and zipped up the hole, disappearing completely from the Green Tara system.

The way the Skat ship manipulated space took my breath away. We were all very still for what felt like a very long time.

Gordy finally broke the silence. "That's a different way to travel."

"There have been reports, up until now unverified, of renegades who are capable of translight travel," Dot said, back to her basic tutor voice.

"Wherever they went, you sure took care of them, Gin," Gordy said.

"Ditto on the praise," Dot's tone shifted to bouncy. "That was faster-than-light thinking, Blazing Bat Girl."

"Bat Girl? What happened to 'My Lady'?" I asked.

"That tag seemed to irritate you. Now, I'm into 20th century television. Meow."

"Why are you making cat sounds?"

Dot said, "Spooky inspired me."

Spooky was nuzzling against Dot's soft edges.

Dot said, "I'm playing one of my all time favorites—Cat Woman. She's a recurring character on the superhero series *Batman*."

"You have time to play your files?"

"I'm designed to multi-task. In any case, I thought it would be wise to take a little leisure time," Dot purred. "You realize, any movement on our part could alert the Skats or anyone else who might be scanning for us. The program's already cued up." Dot started a *Batman* episode, one in which Robin drives the Batmobile.

Gordy said, "My favorite episode."

"Ugh," I lowered my pilot's chair. "I need a nap."

"Purrrfect," purred Dot.

"While we're resting, how about Dot and I look for life signs on Green Tara?" Gordy suggested. "We're close enough, aren't we?"

Dot's light panel twinkled at Gordy. Twinkled! I hated it when they got along and I was the grumpy third. I'd gone from peacefully alone, to having my space invaded. Gordy simply jumped aboard and took control, but I was the one leading the rescue mission for my mother!

On top of hating the fact that Gordy's high energy and good nature eclipsed my own, there was the lingering mystery about the Skat ship. How had it disappeared so completely? Dot had referred to their apparently instantaneous move as *renegades capable of translight travel*. Sure the label *renegade* could stand for any common outlaw, but it implied a band of traitors. That reminded me, Dad had said the Skats couldn't be trusted.

But we'd scared them off. We were in a good position. With plenty of oxygen ... Zap, I was tired ...

⊕

Flight Path to Green Tara

My nap lasted a full twelve hours. Apparently, Dot had insisted I sleep as long as I needed. When I woke, the colonial cruiser was long gone, and the Skats hadn't returned. So, I did a little infinity chase around the plasma cloud where we'd parked. Gordy was dutifully impressed, though I didn't practice my flying skills just to impress him. My moves were equal parts happy dance and systems check. After all we'd been through, my scramjet and I both needed a stretch.

We were close enough to the Tara system for me to chart a precise flight path to Green Tara. I got clearance from Dot, and then aimed the nose of my Blast to our Momo-rescuing destination. Zap! I loved to fly.

The journey to Tara was uneventful. Over the next day and a half, I had Dot regularly check for radiation levels and any other toxins that might be dangerous, but as we'd expected there was nothing unsafe about the Forbidden Zone. The Triumvirate just didn't want anyone traveling through this sector of space. Gordy and I speculated about valuables hidden somewhere in the Zone.

Finally we locked into orbit around the green planet. I watched the locator panel intently. We all did. But we circled the planet three times without finding any sign of human life anywhere. My hopes of finding Momo dropped. Spooky paced back and forth along the dash.

Gordy asked, "What about human made or manufactured objects?"

I didn't have much hope. But, Dot whirred into action and reset the locator parameters. Two white markers lit up, one on the coast and another, larger one, in a forested area on Tara's 45th parallel.

I dropped the Blast into the atmosphere where billowing clouds floated over the vast ocean. Closer to the surface, schools of fish leapt above the waves. A mountainous coast loomed ahead.

I slowed as we approached the first marker. After three days of interstellar travel I was ready to climb out of the tiny coupe and explore. Gordy was always restless, too. We both pressed our noses to the window. On the rocks below, I could see something that looked linear, possibly architectural, but the water licked one side and on the other there was nowhere to land between it and the rocky cliffs. Some hardy plants clung to the iron-red rocks, but the mountains looked inhospitable.

Hoping to find a better landing place, I skirted the coastline for a short distance to the south, but there was nothing that would work. Dottie said it was high tide, so I lifted the Blast up above the peaks and hovered. An arc of colorful light marked a distant area to the northeast.

Gordy and I inhaled, and simultaneously whispered, "Wow."

"That phenomenon of light refraction is called a rainbow." Dot said, "When the daylight hits fine water droplets suspended in the atmosphere, the water acts as a light-splitting prism. A prism physically separates the light into different wavelengths, and we see those wavelengths as colors."

I don't know why this scientific phenomenon had such a calming effect on all of us, but even Spooky's purr grew louder.

Dot said, "The ancients believed that a rainbow was a promise from the Great Spirit of gifts and well-being."

The rainbow was beautiful, but the promise I was hoping to find was the human-made structure. The center point of the bow marked the location of the second white marker. "It may only be a random refuse dump. But if we're lucky, it's a science outpost with records of human activity."

I switched the Blast from hover mode, and flew slowly so we could observe the details of the landscape. We moved through a pass and over a sizeable mountain lake. This was still water, different than the ocean, and a deep color of turquoise like nothing I'd ever seen. What we saw in the distance was a vast carpet of green. From our point of view, the tree canopy stretched inland to the horizon.

"Tara's so green. More intense than what we saw in the orb," Gordy said.

He was right about the color intensity but, even though the overall impression was green, what I noticed at the lake's edge was that the leaves and branches came in every color and variation, from deepest indigo to splashes of bright gold.

We skimmed along just above the treetops. The daylight saturated my eyes and made me light-headed. Gordy started to say something else when suddenly thousands of bright orange birds joined us. I banked north with them, and we became part of a fervent migration.

Gordy was speechless. I was, too. I held the plush side of Dot next to my face and stroked her. We were all enchanted.

The landscape below us dropped away. The treetops were gone and a gorge several kilometers deep opened up below.

A jolt shook the Blast so hard Gordy and I bounced out of our seats. I suppose we should have been buckled in. Then the Blast sputtered and we went into a tailspin. I couldn't reach the controls. "Dot, stabilize." I peeled Dot off my forearm and tossed her onto the console.

But before she could plug in and take control, the Blast plummeted, and Dot slid off the dash. "Oops."

"Don't say, oops. My whole life, you've never said oops." I tried not to panic. "What's happening?"

Dot flashed diagnostic yellow. "Something's clogged the number two engine," she said, hanging from the side of my pilot's chair. "And now our gyro sensors are whacked."

Gordy pulled himself into his co-pilot's seat and pulled back on the throttle. The Blast leveled out about five meters above the riverbed at the bottom of the gorge. "Manual alignment—successful."

"Not bad, for a beginner."

Gordy smiled. I rarely gave him a compliment. Coming from me, *not bad* was a big deal.

I said, "Before we continue, let's blow a reverse air jet through the intake."

"Good idea," Dot said.

I picked her up and sat back in my pilot's seat. We were stable again. Pssssshht. In front of the Blast a tiny wad of goop squirted out and hung suspended in the air jet.

Dot burped. "That's better."

"So what was it?" I asked. "Did we run into one of the birds?"

"A bird like the ones we saw would have been too big to get pulled into the Blast's engine. Even if we'd hit one of the flock and sucked in feathers, those would have burnt up instantly. These remains are still moist, which is why they clogged the intake. It seems likely we ran into an airborne insect." Dot cut off the air jet and the goop dropped.

"You're saying we nearly wiped out in a random encounter with a primitive life form?" I said.

"Welcome to Tara," Dot said.

Gordy smiled. "I like it here."

Zap. My cousin was infatuated with killer insects.

The locator panel beeped and he pointed to a triangular white marker. We were close.

I climbed out of the gorge and locked in our destination again. I decided against rejoining the birds migrating inland. Even though I was curious about their movement patterns, I chose a direct flight path instead. I wanted to avoid the potential dangers of running into any more wildlife.

⊕

Omega II Research Lab

Once we were closer and could read more detail, the scanner said, "Omega II Research Lab." But all I could see was green, green, and more green. As we hovered over our destination, we saw a distinct circular arrangement of vegetation. Inside the circle a variety of large trees were spaced in a fairly regular pattern. These apparently older trees were ringed by a band of low vegetation. Outside the ring, dense woods stretched in all directions.

Gordy said, "It looks like a target with Omega II in the center."

I landed the Blast gently in the open ring just outside the larger trees. According to our instruments, we were steps away from finding a human-crafted structure, but I still didn't see any signs of human activity. If there was anything to be found, we had to search for it on foot.

Dot said the atmosphere was good to go, so I wrapped her around my arm, popped open the cockpit window, and tasted an organic systems atmosphere—*fresh air*—for the first time. The intense combination of sharp and sweet shocked my nostrils and eyes. I felt dizzy.

Gordy jumped down to the planet surface and Spooky leapt after him. Not to be outdone by my younger cousin, I grabbed my back sling filled with bio essentials and followed. Instantly I felt swallowed by the jumble of vegetation. I tripped and said to Gordy, "Careful. The floor's not even."

Gordy hopped about on the springy, wild carpet. "No problem." He did cartwheels around me.

I said, "Gordy. Save your energy."

"It's not supposed to be even, Gin. It's not a floor. It's the ground and it's fun!"

Dot's face lit up. She spoke in her sensei voice, "Young grasshopper knows something of great value: that energy expended with joy creates more energy." The irises of her eyes spun in cartwheels.

"There'd be greater value in finding the research lab." I grumbled and stumbled around the side of the Blast, looking for any kind of marker. And there it was. Remnants of a geodesic dome. Finally, something that made sense. It was incomplete. Apparently most of it had crumbled over time. But I still recognized it. I knew from my studies that a greenhouse dome was the central feature in original terraforming efforts. None of the glass panels were in place, so I easily stepped through the triangular-shaped support struts into what had originally been the inside of the greenhouse. I stumbled again, this time on a clump of flowers. I picked one and studied it. "It smells sweet."

"You're holding a violet," said Dot.

"I like this." I smelled the fragrance again. It had been wildly intense, but now I couldn't detect any smell. "Oh. It's gone."

Dot said, "Violets are known for their flirty scent. In addition to the hydrocarbons that humans recognize as pleasurable, a major component is a particular ionone compound which temporarily desensitizes the nose receptors, thus preventing continued flower scent detection until the nerves recover."

"In other words, go away and come back and it will smell sweet again," I said.

"That is a very good summary," Dot said.

Something annoying buzzed in front of my face. I dropped the flower and swatted the air. "I don't like that."

"Don't hit the bee," she said.

"A bee? Another flying insect?" Zap. The last insect we'd run into had clogged my engine and nearly killed us.

"He might sting you," she said.

"Sting me?" I was horrified.

"In self-defense," she said.

"This place is dangerous." Then I noticed that Gordy had climbed up into a tree. A tree so enormous it might have had a small lab tucked inside it. "Gordy, get down. The gravity on this planet dominates."

"I have discovered the best sport on our new planet. Tree climbing!" Gordy climbed even higher, out onto a branch, well over my head. "I can see everything from up here."

"Dot. Help. Look up. There, where Gordy is." He was going through a particularly clumsy stage of adolescence and I didn't want to see him tumble and break body parts.

Dot said, "That is a very old, sturdy cypress tree. It can easily support his weight."

"I've discovered another best sport: tree swinging!" Gordy swung off the cypress tree branch, landed on the ground and cartwheeled through another set of support struts. "That definitely looks human-made." He pointed several meters in front of where we were to a straight, hard edge beneath moss and leaves, low to the ground and almost entirely masked by growing things. He hopped forward, bent down and pulled some vines away, revealing the sign: *Omega 2 Research Lab.*

The rectangular shape was less than impressive. I said, "It must be a very small lab."

"The facility appears to be largely underground," Dot said.

Gordy walked around the sign and examined what appeared to be a small bluff behind it. "Gin, look." He'd found the entrance, but what used to be the main door was also covered in vines. "If your mom was ever here …." He sounded crushed.

Which was how I felt, too. No one had used this door in a very long time. "We may find clues inside." I helped him pull the vines away, revealing an access code keypad.

He made a quick assessment of the locking system design. "This'll take forever to hack into." Frustrated,

Gordy stripped more of the vines away and tried to pry open the door. Then he pounded it.

Meanwhile, I climbed up the vines and onto the roof, which was also covered with ferns and moss. I tripped again, this time on something that felt stiffer than a fern. I squatted down and pried it up. "Dot, what's this"

"The cover to an air vent." Dot blinked. "The Omega II research lab air vent."

I shouted, "Gordy, up here!"

He scrambled up to the roof, and together we cleared undergrowth from the vent cover. "It's big enough," he said.

"Maybe," I said. But it was dark inside and less than a meter down the vent angled slightly, just enough that it was impossible to see how far down it went. I wanted more information before we just jumped in. "Dot, can we get in this way?"

"The lab's basic security blocks my ability to scan below the surface. From this position all I can detect is a total volume of space. Eleven thousand cubic meters." Gordy dropped a small pebble and we listened to it skitter down the airshaft. The sound grew fainter and then intermittent, but it never actually stopped.

"Sounds like the volume's all straight down. I don't think an endless shaft is the way to go." I looked for another entrance.

Meanwhile, Gordy was fooling around with the vines. He loosened one enough to wrap it around his waist. Spooky scrambled along the vine, headed for Gordy. "This should be strong enough."

"Strong enough for what?" I asked.

Gordy peered down into the open vent. By this time Spooky had crawled onto Gordy's chest. He supported the kitten's bottom with one hand and held onto the vine with the other. "I'm going to get a closer look at the situation." Now I knew what he was planning to do, but before I could stop him he jumped into the vent and disappeared. "Whoa-aww!"

I rushed to the vent. Of course, I couldn't see anything. "Dot, we're going to need a light." I grabbed my own vine—what else could I do?—and slid in after him.

⊕

Inside the Lab

The air vent was a smooth ride. To a point. *JOLT.*

I reached the end of the vine. It snapped and I dropped straight down. CRUNCH! I landed on Gordy's back.

It knocked the breath out of both of us.

In Dot's light I could see Gordy's fine, light hair, stirred by spinning fan blades. Any closer and the tip of his nose would have been sliced off. Neither one of us moved. We watched Spooky scrambling up and then sliding down the curved wall of the tunnel, and the pebble, the one Gordy had dropped from above, bouncing around the exhaust fan blades.

"Now we know why the pebble never stopped moving," he croaked.

I lifted myself off of Gordy's back and he sucked in a deep breath. Dot's beam bounced off of the metal surroundings. At least we were inside Omega II and I could stand up without stooping. I turned around slowly, peering into the dark ventilation tunnels that branched off in every direction. "Which way, Dot?"

Dot said, "They all lead into the underground lab, so any choice is viable."

Gordy said, "I thought your sensors were blocked." I offered Gordy a hand and he sat up.

"We've apparently dropped below the security wall," she said.

I entered the largest tunnel.

"On second scan, I have a more optimum choice." Dot flashed her high beam behind us, into the narrowest tunnel, the one beyond the spinning fan.

I said, "We could base our choice on easy access."

"This tunnel will take us right over the main room of the station," Dot said.

"The command center?" Gordy asked.

"Nothing active. But I detect the largest and most central room," Dot said. "We'll be better oriented if we start our search there."

I could have overruled, and there were obvious logical reasons for choosing another way—dangerous looking fan blades, for example. But Spooky chose that moment to dash between the blades, disappearing into the black tunnel.

Gordy shrugged. "The cat nap's over." He broke off an end of the vine that was still around his waist and stuck it into the fan, jamming the blades. He squeezed through. "Come on, Gin. You're not that much bigger than me."

I hung back. "Dot, if this one goes to the largest room, why is it the smallest vent?"

"The other tunnels route to entire floors." Dot's voice shifted to sensei and she said, "Patience, young one who is wise and also brave. We don't have far to go."

I really didn't want to follow a cat and a boy on my hands and knees. But I did.

As Dot had predicted, we didn't go far before we found ourselves crawling over a soft glow of ambient light. Gordy tugged at a grate between the airshaft and the large chamber of the research station directly below us.

"Ta da!" He held the grate up and grinned.

"Ow! Can't you get that thing off without bashing me?"

There wasn't any place to put it in the awkward, tight space, without hitting my shoulder, neck, or face. Finally, he dropped it and it clattered on the floor below.

"Good thing we're not going for a surprise entrance," I said.

Gordy tied what was left of his vine to the edge of the opening and handed it to me. "Want to go first?"

Of course I wanted to go first. I always took the lead. He lowered me through the vent opening and—oh joy—down among lots of leaves. Dot turned her high beam on, but it didn't help much in the dense foliage. "This is a lab?"

Dot said, "It appears to be a botany lab, which is logical in the context of terraformation."

I dangled from the end of the vine and dropped the last couple of feet to the floor. It felt hard, not like the springy outdoors, but it wasn't smooth and flat like the floor of a colonial cruise ship.

I assumed Gordy would wait for me to get clear before he dropped down. But I'd hardly found my footing when I heard him say, "Uh oh. Watch out!"

I didn't have time to watch for anything before he landed on top of me, and I fell backwards, flat on the floor. CRACK! Everything went dark.

I couldn't breathe. And the back of my head hurt. I was stunned, but fully conscious, and I distinctly felt Gordy sprawled across my lap. "Get off!" I shoved and rolled out from under him. I brushed Dot's plush side. "Dot, are you okay?"

"My high beam lamp's gone. That's obvious. But my other functions feel intact."

Gently, I opened her and spread her out on the floor to examine her.

Gordy crawled over. "Sorry, Dot"

"No problem, Groady."

I hoped Dot's functions really were intact, but I loved her mash-up name for Gordy. "That's perfect. Groady!"

"Gordy," he protested. "Calling me vile names is … "

Dot said, "I have no vile intentions. It's just that, young man, you could use a bath. Even without my headlamp I can see that." And it was true. There was enough ambient light to see that Gordy still had straw stuck in his shirt from the cruise ship, not to mention all the mud and green stains he'd collected since.

By then my eyes had adjusted to the low level of light. Spooky darted among the leaves. We were surrounded by overgrown plants. What might have originally started as neat, controlled specimens in a botanist's dream courtyard, had taken over the floor and the walls. Gordy pointed up, and we gazed at a faux representation of the sky filtered through a thick canopy of trees.

Something rectangular caught my eye, and I reached into the thick undergrowth. I pulled out a thin, flat object about as long as two fingers with handwriting on it. "What's this?"

"It looks like a garden stake, a marker that identifies a plant." Dot's face flickered. "I need to run a deep-level diagnostic and repair. Back in forty winks." She shut her eyes.

I handed the garden stake to Gordy. If I understood Dot, the handwriting on it named the plant next to where we had landed. *Wintergreen.* But it had no other information on it. I pulled the illuminated manuscript from my back sling and looked for the plant listing.

"Wintergreen." Gordy looked over my shoulder and read Great-gran Vera's notes, too. "It's part of the mint family."

That meant it was similar to the peppermint that had settled my stomach. I kept reading, "This one's for sweet breath." I snagged a leaf and nibbled it. Gordy chewed one, too.

While I read the page on wintergreen, Gordy held the garden stake under the plant illustration. "Look at the handwriting." He whispered, "Our five-times-great-grandmother was here."

The handwriting on the stake looked the same as the manuscript. But that was impossible. "There was no space travel this far from Earth in our great-great-great-great-great grandmother's lifetime."

Dot's eyes fluttered open. "There's no *record* of interstellar travel by humans."

"You're awake. Can you compare the handwriting?" I pointed from the manuscript to the garden stake.

"The handwriting is a match," Dot confirmed Gordy's observation.

He continued to examine the small garden stake, running his fingertip along the edge and sniffing it.

I wondered how the stakes had gotten here, and who had planted the garden, and especially if Momo had been here with the same questions.

"Do you think my mother examined these garden stakes?" I asked. "I mean, we should try to establish if she ever made it to this lab."

"I will check for fingerprints," Dot said. "Now, get your paws off."

He gingerly set the garden stake on her scanning pad and asked, "What can't you do?"

"I'm a multi-tasking, multi-purpose custom think-and-jot pad. You know that."

He affectionately ruffled Dot's shag. "Were you able to repair your high beam?"

Dot answered by blinking the beam. Then her bell chimed. "Virginia, I found a match." I crawled back to look at Dot's display: Two matching fingerprints, one from the garden stake and one from a file. The file included a photo of Maureen Bosque, age 27, taken the year she disappeared.

Chills ran up the back of my neck. We'd found physical evidence. I whispered, "That means Momo was here."

"Most likely," Dot said. "In addition to hers and Groady's prints, I found one more."

I stood up. "While I'm looking for more signs of my mother's mission here, search for the person who belongs to the other fingerprint."

"The person?" Dot started searching her data files. She confessed to Gordy, "This is like looking for a needle in a haystack."

Gordy said, "I have an idea."

"You have lots of ideas, Groady."

"Please, don't call me that." Gordy bit his lip.

"Agreed." Dot's lights twinkled. She said, "Who do you suspect?"

I entered a dark corridor where I could no longer hear Gordy and Dot. As I wound down, deeper into the core of the research lab, I noticed two things. One: the corridor became even more overgrown. The carpet of living undergrowth completely covered the walkway. Two: I heard running water–an automatic irrigation system for the underground gardens? AND—make it three things—I heard birds. I wasn't 100% sure if they were live or recordings, but I was surrounded by birdsong.

Questions about my mother haunted me. Did she plant the wintergreen in the herb garden? Would I find any more clues to help track her? When I was little I called her *Momo*. What would I call her now?

As I continued, the corridor grew slightly brighter. Then it widened out into an enormous dome-shaped space where birds flew all about. The jungle tumbled in from the circular sides. The smell wasn't skanky like the livestock pens on the cruiser, but it tingled my nose and the inside of my mouth.

I crawled over a tree root and stumbled, reaching my arms out to break my fall. What I felt against the palms of my hands was smooth. What I saw through curved glass was the face of a sleeping woman.

Her glossy dark hair draped around her face and shoulders, framing her pale face. Her eyelashes, thick with frost, kissed her high cheekbones. Her lips were the color of alabaster. She lay perfectly still inside what looked like a cryonics tube. I wondered if her eyes were green, like mine.

"Momo?"

Could it be? I could hardly remember, but I'd studied the pictures for years. It must be. Maureen Bosque. The missing scientist, lost in space for more than half of my life. Here she was, frozen in a state of suspended animation. I wrapped my arms around the glass tube and held my mother tight.

⊕

⊕

Momo

Some theorize that those in suspended animation can actually hear voices outside their cryonic chambers, but I wasn't thinking about the effect I might have on the woman inside. I was absorbed by what I wished our life had been. I had years of feelings and thoughts and observations to share, so with my cheek against the glass tube I whispered a stream of stories to my frozen mom. Mostly, I told her about the Blast and learning to fly, and the infinity chase and how calm it made me to focus so completely on staying fast and tight.

Gordy gently touched my shoulder. "Gin-Gin?" I felt his warm breath behind me, and he spoke again, softly. "Virginia?"

"She's so much more beautiful than I imagined," I said. "Look at her skin. It glows. All the old pics made her look, I don't know, not glowing. Just kind of flat."

Dot said, "Let's get a more complete look at the situation."

Dot was draped around Gordy's neck. He offered his hand, and I stood up. They led me to a ladder. We climbed to a higher vantage point in the room, on decking where we could see the whole the layout, a star-shaped cluster of identical, clear tubes fanning out from the cryonics freezing unit. Each tube was two and a half meters long and a meter in diameter, ample room for most full-grown adults. They were all empty, except the one with my mother.

Dot replied, "It appears to be a second generation Star Products design. Very reliable."

"You mean, she's still alive?" I understood the basic idea behind a cryo tube and suspended animation. So I wasn't really asking, as much as confirming the situation.

"Oh, yes. Your mother is very much alive."

I patted Dot. "What are we going to do now?"

"I researched the specifications for her cryonic freeze," Dot said.

"Then let's get started," I said.

"There is a danger that we won't be able to reverse the induced hibernation properly," Dot said.

"We'll keep trying to reanimate her until we get the procedure right," I said.

"The tricky part is thawing her out," Dot said, "If it doesn't work the first time, we'll kill her."

I closed my eyes for a moment to clear my thoughts and weigh the options, but there wasn't really much to think about. "As far as I'm concerned, she's been dead and, beautiful as she is, as long as she stays in the tube she's still dead to me."

Gordy nodded, agreeing with my blunt assessment.

Dot said, "I was able to extrapolate 85% of the coding sequence from the machine itself. But we'd have a better chance of success if we could find the records from the time she was frozen."

"Records?" I'd been waiting far too long to be slowed down by the lack of technical specs. I said to Gordy, "You could search the main frame?"

"No, because . . ." Gordy hesitated.

I assumed the central computer required authorization, but Gordy could break any passcode. "Hack your way in."

Gordy shook his head, *no*. "Dot?"

She said, "As far as I can tell, Virginia, I'm the only artificial intelligence here."

"It's a research station. They have to have a library." I expected order and a set of procedures.

Gordy shook his head, *no*.

Dot confirmed, "All data has been removed."

"Removed?" That was impossible. Momo was frozen. She couldn't have removed the records of her frozenness.

As soon as those thoughts crossed my mind, I remembered how easy it had been to disguise our trip into the Zone, even on a corporate colonial cruiser. I was certain that my mother could rewrite historical records so that no one would know she'd ever traveled here, or that she'd gone into deep hibernation here.

"If there're no records, how will we ever figure out how to reanimate her?"

⊕

Reanimation Formula

The risk was too great to make any snap decisions. It was Gordy's idea to eat first and then make an action plan to reanimate Momo. In the kitchen he rifled through the pantry. "Freeze dried mystery snacks." He pulled out several small packets.

"I'm not hungry." I couldn't believe he was interested in feeding his face.

"First, I'm going to feed Spooky. Second, you're insanely hungry, and that's why you can't think straight." Gordy pushed the activation buttons on the F.R.E., food-ready-to-eat, packets and leaned on the counter where I was sitting.

Spooky hopped over my lap, walked along the edge and rubbed up against Gordy. I'd been waiting so long to find my mom, I couldn't believe this pair could act so casually. Gordy let the kitten's tail run between his fingers while he stared at the food packet.

"It's a dud," I said. "It'll never pop."

Pouf! A couple of oversized mugs sprung up, steaming hot. Gordy smiled and read the mug label. "Pumpkin soup." And he added sarcastically, "My favorite." The kitten sniffed at the soup and jumped off the counter top to explore the floor. Gordy punched in another pair of F.R.E.s

I lay down on the counter top. "Don't make any for me. Not till we solve the problem of how to thaw out Momo."

"I want her thawed, too. She's probably the only chance I'll have of tracking down my mom."

So, Gordy knew that his mom was the one who acted when my mom was in danger.

Pouf. Pouf.

"Broccoli!" Gordy made his worst 'yucky' face and pushed the bowl aside.

"How did you know?"

"I read the label." He picked up a mug of the pumpkin soup and tried it. "Oh, not bad." He handed the other mug to me.

"How did you know how your mom disappeared?"

"Uncle Leo told me when I was really little. He said she was the bravest woman he'd ever known. He said when your mom was in danger, my mom flew to protect her."

"Why didn't you tell me?"

"I thought you knew." He looked at me with his big brown eyes, completely innocent. He really thought I'd known my whole life. "I didn't tell you because you never asked."

This was a shocking bit of truth. Every day of my life, in my head, I'd asked the question, *What happened to Momo?* But I'd never spoken it out loud. Not until my last confrontation with Dad. And, even though Gordy's mom was missing, too, I had *never* asked about what had happened to her. The gap in my knowledge was huge.

As soon as we woke up Momo, we'd get the answers. At least, that's what I hoped. "Dot?" I propped up on an elbow. "Let's look at every possible coding sequence for Momo's cryo tube." I sipped the soup while Dot hummed and worked. Basically, we needed to know which compound they used to slow Momo's metabolism, and how quickly she could be brought to room temp.

The traditional method of induced hibernation required bringing the body to room temperature naturally. Turn off the freezer and open the tube. Within a few hours, as her body warmed, she would simultaneously begin to reanimate.

But another compound, developed for security forces and others in crisis mode, required a rapid-action reanimation compound. If Momo had been in a hurry when she went into deep freeze, we'd need to speed up the process so that she wouldn't die of hypothermia when her metabolism kicked up.

Another F.R.E. popped. Gordy examined a blurred label. "I can't tell what this is." He smelled the new food dish. "Mmm."

"Looks like some kind of protein." I caught a whiff of a tangy aroma. "With orange slices." I took a bite. "Mmm, very good."

The kitten returned, meowing, and Gordy offered her some of the protein. Spooky loved it.

Dot's completion bell chimed. Hundreds of coding factors scrolled on her screen.

"That narrows it down," I sat up and examined Dot's findings. "Do you see any patterns?"

Gordy gobbled the protein dish, sharing every third bite with Spooky.

Dot said, "The obvious ones are the markers for weight and sex." Dot highlighted those pairs of the code. "We know, of course that Momo is female, so let's eliminate all the male codes." Instantly, half the codes on Dot's screen disappeared. "I'll use Virginia's stats for Momo's blood pressure, heart rate and other metabolic factors, and apply weight and age differentials."

"Sounds good." I drank the last of my pumpkin soup.

"Put your wrist on my scanner."

I did.

Dot did her best, but the problem was, no matter how many statistics we plugged into the formula, we still didn't have enough information to determine exactly what compound had been used to slow Momo's metabolism. Without that we didn't have enough information to use the right thaw rate to reanimate her.

Dot said, "Without the hard facts, we'll be taking a risk."

"Let's use logic," I said. "Either she went traditional—and we know Momo was a bit of a rebel, so traditional wasn't really her style—or she went with the faster method, which probably fit her impulsive streak."

"What makes you think your mother is impulsive?" asked Dot.

"She didn't plan her mission to Tara very carefully." I felt completely dry. I stuck my head under the water tap and let it run over my face and into my mouth.

Dot spoke evenly. "The letter in the manuscript was not impulsive, Virginia. She left you the clues you needed to find her."

"Sure, we're here. We found her. But where are the clues to help us reanimate her?"

Dot whirred. Spooky crawled across my shoulder and hopped into Gordy's arms.

"Maybe we're asking the wrong question," he said. "I don't think your mother chose the method. The cryo tubes were here in the research lab before she arrived. The question is how did the original terraforming party intend to use reversible metabolic hibernation?"

"That is a very mature analysis, Gordy," Dot said.

Gordy belched. Too late, he covered his mouth.

"Mature?" I tossed Dot over my shoulder. But, as soon as Gordy had asked the better question, we all knew that a crew of terraforming colonists would have opted for the simplest, most natural method. Logic rules. Together, we padded out of the kitchen and into the dark corridor.

At the cryo-tube control pad Dot activated the thaw sequence. She used the one we had chosen, the slow thaw, allowing Momo's body to come up to room temperature naturally. First, Dot turned off the coolant, and the colors in the cryo tube began to shift, indicating the change in temperature. Then Dot reintroduced oxygen inside the tube until the gas matched the breathable air in the lab, ready for when Momo warmed up.

Pink and violet light played over Momo's face. There was nothing else we could do, but wait.

⊕

Tumbling Down

Pink light bounced off the inside of the triple layer of the curved cryo tube and violet light danced across Momo's face and belly. Sitting next to the tube, next to me, Gordy nodded off. Dot hummed quietly on the control pad. We knew the process could take hours, but the precise time was unclear. I didn't want to miss the moment when Momo's tube popped open.

I tried to keep myself awake, but I was so numb I felt like I was floating overhead in the tree canopy, watching myself watch my frozen mother. Interesting: *We have identical hair, straight, black manes of hair. Our heads are an exact contrast to Gordy's soft golden curls.*

I don't remember closing my eyes, but I do remember tumbling down through the leaves.

Dot said, "Virginia, look who's up."

Dot called again and I opened my eyes. At first what Dot said didn't register. I yawned and lazily turned my head to check the progress of Momo's thaw. I blinked a couple of times to clear my focus and, when I saw that the cryo tube was open . . . and empty, I bolted straight up.

My mother was on the other side of the chamber walking around barefoot. "You're awake!"

Momo looked up from the fern she was inspecting and waved back, a bit nonchalantly given the circumstances. "The growth hormones did a number on the ferns."

I pranced to her side and grabbed her. "I didn't think I'd ever see you again. You look great, better than I ever imagined."

Momo was obviously still a little groggy, and the brisk hug threw her off balance. She pulled back and smiled uneasily. "Did you get the field gear ready?"

"Field gear?" I asked. What was she talking about? Wasn't she happy to see me? At least surprised to see me? Something. Anything.

She spoke again, matter of factly, "No reason to wait. Let's get started."

Gordy stepped to my side. He stretched out his hand to his Aunt Maureen, "It's terrific to finally meet you."

"Hello." She winked at me, "Recruiting them awfully young. Of course, you're still young." She looked me up and down. "Have you gotten thinner?"

Thinner? I didn't understand her mother's frame of reference. Sure, I was thin, but I'd put on lots of weight since the age of five.

Gordy jumped in. "Are you hungry?"

"I'm starved."

Gordy said, "Right this way. I think I can find you some towels, too."

"A young gentleman. Thank you." She stumbled. "Oops. Funny. I'll get my legs back soon enough."

I watched my mother sway unsteadily as she followed Gordy through the overgrown corridor. This was an overwhelming moment for me, the one I'd waited for forever, but my mother seemed to lack any desire to connect with me. She barely acknowledged me. This situation called for a major love fest. That would have been awkward in its own way, but at least it would have felt like a real reunion.

I sprinted back to the open cryo tube, and picked up Dot. "What's wrong, Dot? I thought it would be so amazing to finally talk to her. And I really thought she'd want to spend time with me. But, she's acting like no problem. Like no time's passed." I wrapped her around my arm and pressed my face into Dot's soft side.

Dot said, "Remember that, for her, no time has passed. "

"Did you hear what she said? Barely out of the tube and she's looking around for field gear." Momo's reaction was so wrong.

"Coming out of a state of induced hibernation is a disorienting experience. It's reasonable to expect a mental and physical reorientation period."

"So, she won't be herself for a few days?" I stroked Dot. "She didn't even know me!"

"No doubt, the woman is your mother, Maureen Bosque. Her DNA is an unmistakable match. However, when it comes to behavior, humans are notoriously unpredictable."

I followed Gordy and my recently thawed, body-on-the-move, brain-not-yet fully-engaged mother.

Back in the kitchen, my mother inhaled three protein dinners. I popped a fourth F.R.E. and handed it to her as soon as it was ready. She nodded her thanks and consumed that one as fast as she could.

I looked through the doorway into a lounge room where Gordy had wandered after his own multi-F.R.E. meal. He was asleep with little Spooky curled up on his chest. I needed more sleep, too, so I stretched out on the kitchen counter top where I could watch my mother.

I attempted to start a conversation. "So, you asked about field gear."

"I assume we have clear access now," my mother said.

I still didn't understand. "Access for …?"

"For our expedition. Why else did you thaw me out, Celia?"

"Wait. Back up. Celia. I'm not Celia. My name's Virginia."

My mother set her empty bowl down. "Don't mess with me. I still have deep-freeze brain." She stood up and stretched. "I'll do better if I move around some more. How about I collect the field gear?" She asked as if it was a question, but it wasn't. She exited the kitchen, clearly on her own mission.

I curled up in a tight ball. My mother didn't even recognize me, and why would she? The last time she'd seen me I was just a little kid. I shut my eyes to stop the tears. I was so sleepy my body hurt.

I don't know how long I slept, but when I opened my eyes my mother was hovering over me.
"Did you say that you're Virginia?"
I nodded.
My mother pointed into the lounge. "And that's Gordon? Your cousin?"
I nodded again. "Yes." I looked into my mother's eyes. They were sea green, exactly the same shade as my own.
"You look exactly like my sister, Celia. Your . . . Aunt Celia." Her breath was shallow. She asked, "How old are you?"
"Fifteen. I just turned fifteen." I sat up.
Her face wrinkled, and she almost choked on her next words. "You're not a baby anymore. And you're so beautiful." Momo wrapped me up in her arms.
After years of pretending like I didn't care, I felt so safe, I let the tears fall.

⊕

The Problem with Spooky's Eyes

My gaze drifted to where Momo sat absolutely upright on a floor cushion. I was next to her, curled up on a soft lounge chair, and I kept my breathing slow, like I was still sleeping. I wanted to keep this still moment and the way the heat from her hand radiated through my whole body.

Gordy was sprawled on another lounge chair with Spooky nested in his hair. The kitten was the first to move. He stretched and tugged on Gordy's golden curls. With a grunt Gordy rose, stepping carefully over Momo's legs. "Pardon me," he said and he ambled off to the restroom, carrying Spooky across his shoulders.

Momo let go of my hand and said, "He's a surprisingly well-mannered boy." She stood up and tested her balance. Still wobbly, but getting better. "I'm trying to remember, what happened." She went into the kitchen and punched a F.R.E.

Gordy returned and stood in the doorway between Momo and me. He moaned. "Big problem here."

"The problem is you're interrupting," I said. "Momo is finally remembering what happened."

"I don't remember much—just that I was in the aviary hatching birds," Momo said.

"Look." Gordy insisted, holding up Spooky.

"You finally figured out it's too young to be away from its momma," I said, impatient with the distraction.

Momo looked at the kitten closely. "Its eyes are glued shut." She examined white, gooey seepage in and around Spooky's eyes. "They were clear before?"

"Yesterday they were fine," Gordy nodded. "What do we do now?"

"I'm not sure. Dot, do you have Vera's entire encyclopedia?"

"No, I didn't scan pages that are not directly relevant to the mission," Dot said.

She turned to me, "Did you bring Great-gran Vera's manuscript with you?"

"It's in my sling, in the lounge."

My mother took the kitten from Gordy and held it in her arms. "Let's see what we can do for the baby." She stepped into the lounge, with Gordy right behind her.

I didn't understand what the manuscript had to do with Spooky's eyes. And I really didn't understand her priorities. My mother was more interested in cleaning up a kitten's goopy eyes than in getting to know me.

I followed her into the lounge.

Momo combed through Vera's manuscript for the treatment of eye diseases, and she must have seen something she thought would work because she jumped up and took off through the lab garden, Gordy right by her side. I tried to keep up with them. They didn't have any trouble navigating through the hydroponic beds, but I kept stumbling on overgrown plant limbs and the nuts that littered the floor.

Gordy said something, and my mother laughed, a heady musical sound. I slipped on something squishy and ended up on my hands and knees surrounded by roundish purple things. Dot called them plums and suggested I eat one that I hadn't stepped on or smashed in another way. The smell was sickening sweet and I felt nauseated, like another flood-of-tears drama scene was about to erupt. No. That wasn't happening here, crawling on the floor in the muck. I got up and raced through the orchard. I didn't want to be left behind.

Gordy pointed to a plant, 20 centimeters tall with purple-veined leaves and tiny flowers. "Is this what you're looking for, Aunt Maureen?"

She held Great-gran Vera's manuscript next to the plant and compared it to a sketch of the plant called *Eyebright*. "It looks like a match. Virginia, let's show this to Dot."

I peeled back Dot's plush side so she could see. After a quick glance at the plant and the corresponding illustration, she agreed with a chime.

I pulled out the plant's garden stake and said, "But, it's labeled *Euphrasia*."

Dot said, "Despite the name discrepancy, it does appear to be the very same plant. *Euphrasia* is the technically correct name, but the ancients, like your great-grandmother Vera, often called plants by a name that indicated a plant's medicinal uses. *Eyebright* is the colloquial name."

Momo brushed the tops of the flowering plants. "It's an elegant little plant, and Euphrasia is an elegant name. But, I like the sound of Eyebright."

Back in the kitchen I sat on the counter while Momo crumbled the Eyebright flowers into a jar. The general idea was to use the plant to make a medicine for Spooky's eyes. I wondered about Momo's experience making eye medicine. As far as I knew, she wasn't medically trained. She asked me to look for a liter of purified water to make an infusion.

While I found the water, I asked Dot to explain.

"An infusion is a large amount of herb that is brewed in water for a long time," Dot said, as if that explained it.

Momo pulled a clear, glass jar out of the cooking supply cabinet. "Gin Gin, set the water to boil for us."

She called me *Gin Gin,* just like when I was little. Finally, some sign that we were close—or had been. I punched the *boiling hot* button on the water pack. "So, you know how to brew an herb?"

"Not exactly. The instructions are incomplete, as if some of the basic steps were generally understood when Vera wrote the book. But perhaps it really is this simple." She scooped up all the flowers and leaves and stuffed them into the glass jar. When the hot button popped, she poured boiling water over the Eyebright. Momo certainly acted like she knew what she was doing.

"The one thing that's missing is time. The medicinal potency is stronger when you use dried herbs, because the minerals and phytochemicals are more accessible. But drying the leaves would take several days, and Spooky needs something for his eyes sooner than that. So we'll work with what we have. Now we let it soak." Momo covered the jar and left the kitchen.

I stretched out on the counter and watched the Eyebright brew. Inside the jar there were flowers, leaves, and water. Not much to look at.

Later, after the infusion had brewed and cooled, Gordy entered. "What do you think, Aunt Maureen, will this work?"

I opened my eyes—apparently, I had been napping—and watched the two of them.

Gordy handed Momo a small glass jar with a dropper lid. She took the jar and smiled—the kind of smile that made the corners of her eyes turn up. It was the first time I'd seen that look since we'd brought her out of cryo.

"Perfect," she said and ruffled Gordy's hair.

Zap! Now she was calling Gordy *perfect*.

Momo made a funnel with some gauze and poured the liquid from the infusion jar into the smaller one Gordy had found.

"This isn't full strength yet, but it may soothe your kitten's eyes. It certainly won't hurt him." She screwed the eyedropper into the small jar, and the two of them went into the lounge where the sick kitten was napping. I rested my cheek against Dot's plush side. "We don't even know if this plant medicine works."

"That's true. We only have anecdotal evidence from ancient Earth." Dot spoke softly, "While a cure is not guaranteed, it is my general philosophy to trust the process."

I mouthed Dot's words without making a sound, "Trust the process?" I thought Dot would call for precise logic and empirical evidence in the pursuit of science.

Instead, Dot spoke resolutely, "When faced with the unknown, even if the outcome is uncertain, a true Bosque will continue to act with unwavering intention. In short: Believe. And act on what you believe."

Gordy held Spooky on his lap and my mother dropped the Eyebright infusion into the kitten's eyes. Gordy was trusting the process—no problem. I watched the cozy scene from the doorway, feeling more and more left out.

⊕

The Eyebright Solution

"Before the end of the day the Eyebright had cleared the goo away from Spooky's eyes," I said to Dot. Of course, she already knew this information, but I was recording my Dear Dot log—something I did every day, usually. Lately, I'd been so caught up in the rescue mission that I'd gotten out of the habit. Now, here on Tara with Momo, I was trying to sort things out, and it made sense to record my thoughts.

I paced in a small room off the lounge that I'd claimed as personal space and continued my log.

> ... This morning when we woke up, after eight hours without the Eyebright, Spooky's eyes were glued together again. Momo added another ingredient with antiseptic properties, and Gordy helped her prepare the new infusion. Spooky's not completely healed but, as long as Gordy keeps applying the drops, he seems to be getting better. Momo said with the support we're giving him, his body will be able to

shake off the infection. ... Maybe now that the kitten's better, she and I will ...

I stopped recording my Dot log mid-thought, as soon as I realized my mother was standing in the lounge doorway.

"Maybe we'll what?" she asked.

"Maybe we'll learn to knock before entering." I closed Dot. I didn't know how long my mother had been listening in to my personal thoughts.

"You even talk like Celia. You move like her and think like her." My mother came inside my room and sat down. "Thawing me out took courage."

She may have thought she was giving me a compliment. True, I had been desperate for her to notice anything about me, but at this point I didn't want any of her sweetness. She obviously liked Gordy more than me. And she was still comparing me to her sister, Celia. That didn't feel like a compliment. It felt more like a slam. "When Celia left you here, she didn't exactly make things easy."

Gordy entered and made my room feel even more crowded. "I heard you talking about my mom. I know you haven't had much time to think, Aunt Maureen, but I want ..." Gordy paused for a painfully long time.

"I want to find Celia, too. But, I don't know why she's not here." She took Gordy's hand. "All night, I've been thinking about what happened, but I don't remember anything that will help us find her."

"What's the last thing you do remember?" Gordy asked.

"I remember Celia called to warn me I was under investigation. She said a bounty hunter was tracking me."

"A bounty hunter?"

"That's what she thought. I never encountered the bounty hunter, but … " Momo paused, tilting her head, touching her forehead to his.

I couldn't stand to watch them together. The tenderness was sickening sweet. "Two things," The words slipped out before I even knew what I was going to say. "One. Both of you, knock before entering. Two. Gordy, you're just sucking up to my mother because you think riding her comet tail will take you straight to your mom." I heard the meanness in my voice, and Gordy definitely looked hurt.

My mother said, "Gordy, I believe Celia risked her life and erased her trail to protect me and Green Tara. I also believe she's still alive, in hiding. We'll find her. It may not be as soon as we want, but we will find her. For now, please give me and Virginia some time to talk alone."

He nodded and backed out. She turned to me and her eyes hardened. "I expect more from you."

"More what?" I snapped back.

"More basic courtesy, to begin with. Gordy deserves your kindness. And I expect more enthusiasm for our mission. You were such a fierce little girl. Now you just want everything to be easy. You think that will make you happy?"

"What's wrong with being happy?"

"Nothing's wrong with happiness. But if you're only concerned with personal happiness, you're thinking like a self-serving Triumvirate clone. Didn't Dot and your father teach you there is more to life? For a Bosque what is important is ALL of LIFE."

I hadn't expected a lecture on ALL of LIFE. What I had expected from my mother was carefree together time. Instead, when we were alone she made me feel guilty for not being a martyr, like she'd been in her cryo tube for years. How had that helped the Bosque mission?

She stood up, and I braced myself for more guilt. Instead, she said, "I'm starting to remember more."

Momo wandered out of my room, through the lounge, and down a winding corridor.

I found Gordy and apologized for being heartless. I wanted to find his mother, too, and someday I knew we would.

⊕

In the Aviary

Gordy and I followed Momo into a light-filled chamber with a vaulted ceiling.

This was the aviary, the most dramatic location inside the lab. It was alive with an incredible variety of bird species. The three of us paused to listen to the musical voices. The sound made my scalp tingle.

Momo spoke slowly and carefully. "I was working with the bird incubators and the recently hatched baby cardinals. They're lovely song birds. The adult males have brilliant red plumage." She walked along a row of empty glass tanks, stopped at the third one from the end, and opened the incubator lid. She shifted the nesting material around, but there was nothing else inside the small tank. "I must have released the birds. I wish I could remember seeing them learn to fly."

This was disturbing. My mother was wishing she could remember seeing birds learn to fly. *What about me? Why are birds more important than me? Don't you wish you'd seen me, when I was learning to fly?* But I didn't ask the pounding questions. What I said instead was, "If a bounty hunter was after you, hatching more birds sounds like a ridiculous thing to do. There are plenty of birds on this planet. When I was flying my scramjet, I nearly collided with a flock of them."

"You're right about the bird population on Tara," she said. "But learning how to hatch new birds is part of my training for the primary mission."

"Primary mission?" I blurted.

"Virginia, I mean *the mission*, the one that is larger than either one of us." A pair of small birds with gold bands of color around their necks fluttered to a nearby seed tray. "I needed to learn how to hatch birds so that someday we can return to Earth and repeat the process there."

She pointed to a nest in an overhead branch and climbed up onto the counter to check inside it. "Too bad. This one's empty." She stepped across the counters and peered into another nest. "Here are three eggs. You'll see. The newborns start out so weak. Without a feather."

This whole conversation had gone off on a tangent. My mother was still talking about bird propagation, which was completely irrelevant.

"I remember now." She sat on the counter. "When she called Celia and I discussed using the cryo chambers to hide. She suggested I mask my human life signs by going into a deep freeze, and when the bounty hunter and other security forces were tired of looking for me, she'd come to revive me. That obviously didn't happen." Her voice cracked with emotion. "I should remember where she said she'd go to hide."

"Don't worry, Aunt Maureen," Gordy said. "We'll figure it out."

I was grateful Gordy was nice to her. I changed the subject. "Momo, how did all this get here before you did? I mean the incubators, the eggs to put in the incubators and ... everything."

Momo answered, "You two know that Great-gran Vera's vision was to create a sanctuary for natural life?"

"We've seen her manuscript and understand why it was important to protect the wildlife," Gordy nodded. "But here? How is that possible? People of her generation didn't travel outside the prime solar system. They'd barely gotten beyond the asteroid belt."

"You know your history." She moved through the incubator aisles, and Gordy followed her. "It's true. Vera didn't come here in a space ship. She and her fellow explorers traveled here through hyperspace."

"Hyperspace? Wow! I thought hyperspace transport was only theoretical," Gordy said.

"You're saying, our Great-gran Vera built a hyperspace transport system?" That I found hard to believe.

"No, she didn't build it," she said. "I don't think anyone ever figured out where the hyperspace jump point came from—who built it and where they've gone—any knowledge about the original star travelers has been lost."

The cryo freeze had done more than make my mother a little forgetful. Now she was sounding delusional. People had always speculated about other intelligent life in the galaxy, and since the earliest space flights there had been hope to make contact. But no concrete evidence of another race of beings had ever been officially documented. And the whole bit about hyperspace travel … And a jump point? My mother was supposed to be a scientist, not a science fiction geek.

"I'm going to go pack." My mother said, hopping off the counter.

"You're packing for . . .?" I probed.

"A field expedition," she said. And without a backward glance she left the aviary, with Gordy close behind.

⊕

Earth Restoration Alliance

I caught up with Gordy, and we both followed my mother as she wound her way through the corridor, heading back toward the living area. "Aunt Maureen, did you say that our Great-gran Vera came here to Green Tara?" Gordy phrased it like a question, but he clearly didn't have any doubts.

"She was one of the explorers who first came here from Earth via hyperspace." My mother added matter-of-factly, "The jump location is marked by distinctive rock formations with keyhole openings, archways large enough for human passage." She stepped into her personal room, took off her slippers and sat down to lace up a pair of rugged boots.

Meanwhile, I needed a rational perspective, so I opened Dot's face and whispered to her, "Have you seen an ancient *hyperspace transport keyhole in a rock*—either here on Green Tara or in the prime solar system?"

Dot twinkled and opened up a pair of images.

Unbelievable. Dot was showing me pictures of geological formations.

Alongside the rocks, Dot displayed a corresponding star chart and planetary map. Gordy peered over my shoulder.

I asked, "Dot, where did you find these?"

"In the back of your Great-gran Vera's manuscript," Dot said. "You told me to scan for anything that was relevant. The one on the left is the prime solar system, with a map of a southwestern coastline on Earth." Dot highlighted the Earth map, and said, "This is a continent called South America. The chart on the right is the Tara system, with a map of a southwestern coastline on this planet."

Momo stepped to my side and pointed to a circle on Dot's screen. "Please, magnify."

Dot zoomed in on the Tara map. Blocky handwritten letters, much different than the script in Vera's encyclopedia of plants, marked the location *Omega II*.

"That's where we are now," Momo said. "At the second terraforming station that George built."

"George?" I asked.

"George Bosque, Vera's husband."

Gordy said, "Our five-times great grandfather?"

She nodded and continued, "Our Great-grandfather George was one of the first astronauts who traveled beyond the asteroid belt. He and a team of explorers landed on a Saturn moon named Iapetus, and there they found a key and a star chart. It pointed to the location of a hyperspace jump point on Earth, which led directly to another jump point here on Green Tara."

"That sounds convoluted." Momo and Gordy both turned and stared at me as though I'd said something really stupid.

Momo pointed to the map again, to a keyhole archway notched in a small island just off of the southwest coast. Near it was a triangle labeled *Omega I*. "This was their first terraforming station. When they arrived, Green Tara was devoid of life, but it had water and the climate was right. George and Vera brought in plant life from the Earth's oceans to generate an oxygen atmosphere, and here at the estuary, where the river meets the sea, they incubated fish eggs."

"And once they transplanted ocean life, they built a second terrestrial lab and brought other kinds of eggs and seeds here." Gordy pointed to the *Omega II* circle on the map.

Finally, I understood how it was all connected: the legend, the terraforming dome outside that had once solidly ringed the Omega II station, the bird incubating tanks in the aviary, and the remarkable life that now thrived here. It was so obvious to me now.

I said, "Green Tara is a wildlife sanctuary. Is that why you came here?"

"Yes." Momo nodded. "Vera had already recorded the manuscript that we've inherited, hoping that they would discover a way to save the natural life on Earth. Then George and his crew discovered the hyperspace connection between the two worlds. Earth and Tara are two uniquely suited planets, each with water and temperate climates and each with an iron crystal core."

Gordy whispered, "Tara has an iron crystal core?"

"Yes, very much like Earth's. It's an unusual geological phenomenon, though not unique. It seems to be the hyperspace connection. But we're getting into conjecture. We still don't know how it works."

"So Vera and George knew about Tara, and there were others involved?" I asked.

"There was a small exploration crew. From their first discovery, they knew they had found a place they could use as a wildlife sanctuary, a place where they could protect living plants and animals from extinction and keep them free from Triumvirate Corporation control. They seized the opportunity. And, of course, they all made a vow to keep the entire mission a secret."

Gordy whispered, "I've heard of the Earth Restoration Alliance."

"Yes, the early astronauts and the scientists who worked with Vera were the founders. Most people laughed at the idea, said it wasn't necessary. But our ancestors and their loyal friends with the E.R.A. made a series of expeditions. First with phytoplankton, then with fish, then here at Omega II with terrestrial plants and insects, and finally with birds."

Spooky jumped into Gordy's lap. "No mammals?" he asked.

"Movement through the portal was always tricky. They couldn't risk the Triumvirate discovering their mission. One person at a time, they managed to carry thin body armor filled with frozen eggs through hyperspace to Green Tara. But they didn't solve how to populate the new planet with mammals before access was completely cut off." Momo picked up a few articles of clothing.

"Then that'll be our task, to bring mammals here," Gordy said.

I was baffled why he thought this was now our mission. I said, "We're a couple of centuries too late."

"This kitten's not the only mammal in the galaxy," Gordy said.

Before I could formulate all the reasons why returning to the colonial cruise ship to retrieve more mammals was a bad idea, my mother said, "I'm going to get my gear." She left, with Gordy close behind.

I sat in the lounge, alone with my thoughts, which were less coherent thought and more a swirl of conflicting emotion. I wanted to be loyal, but I also wanted to hold a grudge about Gordy being so eager while I was being so cynical, and I didn't know how to do both at once.

⊕

Packing for a Field Expedition

I followed my mother and Gordy to a large supply closet where things were organized and labeled. "You said, you're getting your gear?"

"Yes." My mother pulled out a backpack from behind a stack of irrigation hose. She poked through more supplies, and selected an assortment of small tools from a shelf. "I'm going on a field expedition, to harvest what we need for Earth restoration."

"What can you do after all these years?" I asked.

My mother didn't even look up to answer me. She was examining a variety of containers. "I'm planning to collect the samples. That's the next step in our mission."

"You keep talking about our *mission*," I said. "I thought finding you was the mission."

"Are the oceans of planet Earth still dead?"

"More or less, but we can't repair the oceans of a planet that's light years away."

My mother turned and looked me in the eye. "It's our job to take the phytoplankton back to Earth and start the process of renewal."

"I believe that our ancestors established this wildlife sanctuary, and obviously life is thriving here," I said. "But why would you want to go back to Earth?"

"There are humans scattered all over the galaxy who need a viable home."

"And we're on it!"

"Gin. Earth is central to who we are. Even if we ignore the deep, deep longing that resonates in every human, even though it's been many generations since anyone was born there, think about those left behind. The refugees on Mars are desperate for a home where they can breathe freely, and for them that can only mean the planet Earth."

I didn't feel as selfless as my mother, and I didn't believe we could pull off saving any planet from environmental ruin, particularly not one in another corner of the galaxy—no matter what Dot had said about the ideal of believing, capital *B*, and acting on belief. But I was beginning to understand why restoring the original planet was so important to her.

"Momo, where are the samples of phytoplankton that you need?"

"The coast."

"The coast?"

Gordy said, "The coast is where land meets the ocean."

"I know what it means," I said to him.

He apparently already knew about the next step of our mission, because he slipped an armload of FREs into my mother's backpack. Then, he tried on a backpack for himself.

My mother said, "Not this time, Gordy. This is my job."

"But Aunt Maureen!"

Gordy was right. I planted my fists on my hips and told her, "Don't even think about going without us." As crazy as her mission seemed, she was obviously determined, and I wasn't going to let her go alone.

"No. If I lose any more family on Green Tara, I'll give this lovely planet an unfair reputation." Nobody laughed. She said, "Don't worry, Virginia. Collecting the samples won't take me that long."

"The last time you said that, you disappeared for my whole life!"

Gordy protested, too, "Aunt Maureen, the ocean's over two-hundred kilometers from here."

"That's why I'm taking overnight gear." She rolled up a couple of polymer blankets and tied them to her backpack.

Gordy said, "Then hand me a blanket, too."

"No. There's nothing for you to pack." My mother used her this-is-a-non-negotiable-decision tone of voice. "You two, stay here."

"Small point: Whatever craft you used to get to Omega II is long gone. And as far as my scramjet is concerned, you—Mother—are not checked out on it. Whereas, I have logged more than enough hours of flight time to get us from here to the ocean and back safely."

My mother stood up and this time, though her mouth didn't turn up into a smile, her green eyes were shining, and I clearly saw the way they crinkled at the corners. "So, you're an expert pilot now."

I thought it was obvious that my flying skills had gotten Gordy and me to Tara. But she might have thought I'd used auto-pilot all the way from interstellar space and into orbit, and even used it to land safely on the planet surface.

My chin rose. "I am an expert pilot, and I'm flying you to the coast," I said.

Gordy stood right next to me. "I'm going, too."

I reinforced our position by stepping a little wider, my arms still akimbo, like the two of us could keep her penned in the closet until she agreed. "We're not losing you, a second time," I said.

My mother said, "That's settled, then. Let's all pack."

"What's to pack? It won't take us long to fly and most of my things are still in my Blast."

"Your Blast? I like the sound of that." She pulled out one more pack and tossed it to me. "In the wilderness it's good to be prepared."

⊕

⊕

Venturing Into the Wilderness

Just inside the main door to the research station my mother tapped the panel keys. "Let's see if I remember the pass code." The door slid to the right.

We all stepped outside. The Tara sunlight fell in patches across my skin, warm and energizing. As lush as the indoor gardens were, they were no match for what was outside. A canopy of tree branches and leaves towered above us.

When we'd landed on the surface, I'd been so intent on finding Omega II on the ground that I hadn't realized the enormity of the surrounding trees. I could see the shiny red hull of my Blast and the tree trunk closest to it was easily five times its size.

"This way," Gordy pointed toward the Blast. "It's a great ride, Aunt Maureen. You'll love it."

Once again, I felt envious of Gordy's easy connection with my mother. I wanted a fresh start with her, a little private bonding time. I said to Gordy, "It'll be a little tight with three of us. Maybe you should stay here while we jet around doing important save-the-old-world stuff."

"You've tried to leave me behind before, and it doesn't work," Gordy said.

"I agree. Let's stay together." My mother marched briskly across the old greenhouse plot and toward the Galaxy Blast.

I tugged on Gordy's arm. "Don't you want to stay and play nurse the kitten?"

Gordy froze. "Spooky! Be right back." He spun around and almost knocked me down as he raced back to the lab.

I'd assumed Spooky was tucked inside his vest. Apparently not. "Momo?" I called.

My mother paused about halfway between the lab and the Blast.

"Gordy will be right back, so I thought we could chart our course." I opened Dot's face flap and said, "Dottie, we're going to need that map again." This was my chance. Navigation was my best subject. I was sure Momo would be impressed with my skill. I sprinted toward her. "We've already found the location of Omega I, so the latitude and longitudinal destination is a given. But ..." Momo looked at me intensely, and the outdoor light made her eyes look like deep pools of water. As deep as the ocean we'd flown over when we'd first arrived on Tara.

"Sounds like you have a question," Momo said.

"The only real question about our course is altitude. I'd like to fly low enough to the surface to collect more detailed information about the topography."

"Excellent thinking," Momo said. "Especially when we near the ocean."

Dot said, "Shh. listen, girls."

Classic. I finally had a few moments and a real conversation going with Momo, and Dot was intruding, telling us to pay attention to wilderness sounds. "Dot, hold that thought." I started to close her flap.

She interrupted, "I know you two have a lot of catching up to do, but I've picked up a signal."

"What kind of signal?" Momo asked.

"A count down." Dot was scanning like crazy, and she sounded distressed. "But, as the lab's central computer memory is gone, I can't figure out exactly where it's coming from."

"When did the countdown start?" Momo asked.

Dot said, "Ten seconds after we exited the station."

"The count?"

"Precisely 1:33, 1:32, 1:31."

The grasses rustled around the perimeter of the clearing, and I heard a strange scraping sound.

"Back-up," Momo said. "Back towards the station."

I followed instructions. "Dot, what's at the end of the countdown?"

"Undefined," Dot said.

"Give me an educated guess," I said.

"A countdown often involves an explosion or an ignition sequence," Dot said.

"Ignition?"

"As in a lift-off rocket for a large aircraft," she explained.

"The research lab isn't getting ready for lift-off, is it?"

"Not likely," She said.

"Gin Gin!" Momo waved me closer. "Time check."

I moved next to her, held up my arm and we read Dot's panel—:10, :09, :08. The ground rumbled. It reminded me of the air exchange rumble of the colonial cruiser, and I realized how quiet Green Tara had been without the constant mechanical engine noises of a space vessel This rumble I heard *and felt beneath my feet* was radically different than the natural planet sounds. I held my breath.

Gordy burst through the doorway with Spooky wrapped around his neck. "Look, his eyes are better!"

Way to focus, Gordy.

He stumbled and collided with us, and I ended up on the bottom of the pile. All I could see from under Momo's shoulder was Dot's screen. ":02, :01, :00."

KARUUSHSHSHHHHHH!

The concussion of air flattened my ears.

Gordy, apparently unruffled by the overwhelming sound, said, "Awesome!"

My mother rolled off of me and looked up. "It's beautiful!"

"Now we know," Dot shouted over the crush of air. "The countdown led to the pressurized dome sequence."

I shouted over the roar, "What dome?"

"The dome of pressurized air," my mother waved her arm in an arc overhead, "Elegant design, isn't it?"

The air shimmered over the tree canopy. I also noticed Momo's hat had fallen off her head and was hanging by a chin strap around her neck. Her thick black hair, which normally hung flat and straight to her shoulders, danced around her face. The wild look suited her perfectly.

"I knew about the dome, but wasn't sure if it was still operable," Momo said.

Dot whirred. "The air composition and pressure is essentially the same as the atmosphere, except at the perimeter, where the air jets are located."

Momo explained, "Much larger than the original greenhouse, this dome was designed to serve the terraforming effort until there was enough oxygen in the planetary atmosphere outside the dome to support the birdlife. I doubt the air pressure dome has been turned on in a very, very long time."

"So when we opened the door, we triggered the air compression jets." Gordy said.

"Must have," she nodded. "I wish I'd known to turn off the dome formation sequence before we stepped outside. Thankfully, no real harm done."

"No harm. Except ..." The branches and leaves shook violently above my landing spot. The shiny red hull wasn't on the ground anymore. It was four meters higher. "Except my Galaxy Blast has become a tree ornament." I walked to the edge of the clearing, near where I'd landed, and looked up. My Blast hung upside down, draped among the limbs of the old cypress tree.

⊕

⊕

Upside Down in the Montezuma Cypress

The Blast was hanging upside down in the same tree Gordy had climbed when we first landed. Dot tried to reassure me that the tree was strong enough to support the weight of my small, but substantial, scramjet. Reading from Great-gran Vera's notes, she said, "This isn't just any cypress. This is a Montezuma Cypress or Ahuehuete, which translates as *old man of the water*." The tree was tall and obviously old, and the defining feature was its stout trunk. But I was upset my Blast was in the tree, whatever the variety, no matter how strong the supporting structure.

Gordy slipped out of his backpack and climbed the tree to get a better look at the ship. He shook his head. "Both fore and aft hatches are pinned."

"The ship would have made the trip a lot faster," my mother said.

"The trip?" My Blast was stuck in a tree and my mother was talking about her trip to the coast. "We're stuck on an uncharted piece of dirt, and you're still thinking about your expedition?"

My mother seemed surprised that I was questioning her. She spoke slowly, "Virginia, our only choice is to take the next right action. Gordy, go back to the kitchen and pack as many F.R.E.s as you can find." He nodded and scooted back inside. She turned to me again. "Now, let's plan our route. Ask Dot to pull up George's map."

While I opened Dot and spread her out on the ground, my mother adjusted a flexible PIRSD around her own forearm. It wasn't nearly as sleek as Dot, nor as colorful, but it was definitely another custom TODD model, a Transportable and Omniscient Data Device.

"Wake up, Zoe." Momo's PIRSD screen brightened, and she gave her first command. "First of all, can you turn off the pressurized dome?"

The air jets went silent and the vegetation around the perimeter stopped shaking.

"Thank you." Momo held her arm next to mine. "Dot, meet Zoe."

Dot stared at the blank screen. Then Zoe opened her eyes and looked at Dot.

Dot said, in her friendliest, Southern comfort voice, "Hey, cousin."

"She won't answer, Dot, but she's not being rude," Momo said. "Zoe doesn't have a voice."

Fascinating. The lack of voice for Momo's PIRSD seemed odd given how verbal Momo was. Zoe must have been a first generation prototype—designed even before Dot.

Momo said, "Let's compare maps of the Tara coastline."

I opened Great-grandfather George's map on Dot, while Zoe shimmered and a very similar map appeared on her screen.

"Zoe made this map when we arrived on Tara," Momo said. "How does it compare to George's?"

Dot retrieved Zoë's map and layered it on top of Great-grandfather George's historical map.

Meanwhile, Gordy reemerged from the lab with his backpack brimming with F.R.E.s. He looked over my shoulder and examined the two maps, alongside Momo and me. Some of the features were exactly the same, but a western peninsula and an island near the Omega I symbol were now covered or partially covered by ocean water. "The coast line is radically different here," he pointed out.

My mother tenderly traced the keyhole that George had drawn so long ago. "The plan was to return to Omega I, find the portal, and reactivate the connection."

I interrupted her fantasy, "When we flew over this area, there wasn't anything like a keyhole arch or a research station. All we saw were a few metal racks."

Gordy said, "Maybe George's map is off."

"I think his map's accurate for his time. It's likely the coastline has changed. Remember, during the generations of space travel on the cruise ship—including multiple acceleration rates at near light speed and accounting for the elasticity of time and space—many more years have passed in planetary time."

Gordy said, "I know the theory, but I hadn't thought it through. I mean I hadn't thought about how it's affecting us. We've never been on a planet!"

"Here's a quick physics and geography lesson rolled in one. Over interceding time—planetary time—I suspect a combination of seismic activity and ocean storms have eroded the coastline here." Momo pointed to the Omega I location. "I hope I'm wrong, but I'm afraid the keyhole arch, and with it the hyperspace jump point, has been destroyed."

Which brought up a fundamental question. I asked, "How are we supposed to transport the phytoplankton to Earth, assuming the microscopic green sea stuff is still alive?"

"Oh, it's alive. We wouldn't have the abundant level of oxygen on the surface of Green Tara without it." Momo closed Zoe and put her floppy, brimmed hat back on.

"What difference does that make? Earth's light years away."

"Has your father been working on trans-light speed technology?"

"What does that have to do with mission impossible?" Then I admitted, "Yes. The day before we jumped ship Dad was demonstrating his new faster-than-light communication system to some upper-crust investors."

"That's Leo. He'll get us to Earth."

"Dad? He's too scared to leave the cruise ship. Besides, communication signals are different than physical transport."

But Momo wasn't listening. She tossed me a canteen.

"I always assumed you would embrace our family dream. The commitment has held for seven generations now, with each person acting on faith that the next in line could and would solve the next challenge." Momo leaned forward and whispered, "Even if you can't support the E.R.A., think of Gordy and what it would mean to him."

"I don't follow," I said.

My mother stopped sorting gear. "Gordy's mother risked her life for this. The best way to find her now is to complete our mission, because she's watching for signs from us. She'll know when we restore Earth, and she'll find us."

My mother shouldered her backpack, referred to Zoë's guidance device, and started walking west.

Gordy, obviously impressed by the lure-his-mother-out-of-hiding strategy, put on his backpack.

I said, "My mother's got freezer burn of the brain. We can't follow her."

"Things won't get any better if we just sit here and cry," he said. He turned away from me to follow her, and Spooky raced after him.

For my whole life I'd wanted to know what my mother was really like, and since the discovery of Great-gran Vera's manuscript I'd wanted to know more about her mission—enough to understand the passion that had inspired her willingness to risk everything. But, I hadn't counted on doing exactly what Dad had warned me *not* to do, becoming part of a family quest.

I yelled after Gordy, "I hate it when you act noble."

He glanced over his shoulder and shrugged. But he didn't slow down.

I didn't like being left behind, so I followed their lead.

⊕

Our Trek Through the Wilderness

Gordy and my mother fell asleep as soon as they hung their hammocks. But I couldn't rest. The shifting smells out in the so-called fresh air kept invading my nose.

I heard a giggling whistle that made the hairs on the back of my neck raise up. Dot identified the sound. It was a bird, specifically a loon, calling to its mate. Once the birds stopped calling to each other, other wildlife took over the nighttime airwaves. Dot told me to shut my eyes and pretend the incessant insect drone was the mechanical rumble of an air exchange system.

Then her screen went dark.

I held my breath, wondering how I would manage a trek across a wildlife sanctuary.

We continued our expedition early the next morning, walking through a dense forest and across a rushing stream. My mother and Gordy hopped from rock to rock and made it to the other side without getting their socks wet. I slipped on the moss and ended up soaked.

"She walks too fast," I grumbled to Dot. "I feel like I'm being dragged on a leash by a mad scientist on her sacred mission."

Dot said, "That sounds familiar. You used to say the same thing about your dad. I am, of course, referring to the mad-scientist-on-a-sacred-mission label."

I started to say something, but before I could think of a clever comeback, and completely without warning, tiny insects swarmed every millimeter of my exposed skin, including my eyes and tongue. I was surrounded. I couldn't swat fast enough. Zap! I ran through the cloud, but couldn't escape. They followed me!

By the time I caught up with Gordy and my mother, the cloud had dissipated. So my distress must have seemed overblown. Gordy laughed, and my mother seemed to think the flying insects, *gnats* she called them, were only a minor inconvenience. But I had to breathe, so not only was I wet and uncomfortable, now my nose was clogged with nasty gnats.

On the second day we broke through the forest edge. My mother was first to step into the full sunlight, and she stopped and opened her canteen for a drink of water. Gordy did the same. When I finally caught up I saw what lay ahead, a vast plain, and beyond it mountains.

My mother said, "It'll take us today and tomorrow to cross to the foothills, and another two to climb the crest."

"Four more days?" I whined. I'm not proud of it, but the ordeal had reduced me to whining like a little girl.

"We've been gaining altitude since we left the lab. But up ahead is an easy straight stretch." She closed her canteen. "Let's do it."

My feet were hot and swollen. But the others ignored my pain and struck out across the open plain. I struggled to catch up. What had happened to all the cozy bonding time? Momo joked around with Gordy up ahead and pointed out things to him along the way. But for me—nothing. Instead . . . the trek went on and on.

⊕

⊕

No Water for Personal Hygiene

Because it was summer, the nights were incredibly short, so the sleeping periods were never long enough. Usually Gordy needed lots of sleep, but the whole adventure had charged him up, and he was ready to go at first light. On the third day of our trek I was exhausted, more exhausted than I'd ever been my whole life.

A shower might have helped wake me up, but we were far between water sources. That meant we were in conservation mode. The water we carried was limited to drinking only. No personal hygiene use. Major irritation. I rolled off my hammock and landed on my hands and knees in the dirt. Zap. I wiped the dust off my hands and onto my pants.

Breakfast was a thrilling repeat of orange-flavored protein. Gordy joked, "No chance of scurvy on our mission."

I groaned. How could he be so cheerful?

We settled into our typical arrangement: My mother in the lead, Gordy following closely with Spooky tucked under his arm, and me trailing.

Late in the afternoon, after walking across the endless open plain, we dropped down into a basin. Sulfur gasses bubbled up in noxious-smelling pools, and steam vents burped in random locations on an unpredictable schedule.

Dot warned us that a water geyser was about to blow a few steps away, and we scrambled over rocks to safety. Moments later the geyser shot scalding water twenty meters in the air. I was the last to crawl around a boulder that shielded us from the spray, and my ankles were stung by the hot mist. In other circumstances, I would have been fascinated by all the geological activity and thrilled to continue exploring. As it was, I couldn't wait to escape the boiling geyser field.

The climb out of the basin was hot and steep, and I fell further behind. The lowering sun was directly in my eyes. I kept stumbling on every little stone. Did I mention how tired I was? I whispered to Dot, "Is it possible to sleep and walk at the same time?"

"It's impossible for a human to do both consciously," Dot said.

"I hear one of your 'buts' coming on."

Right on cue she said, "But, theoretically, once you're asleep you can start walking—subconsciously, of course. It's called sleepwalking."

I didn't know what Dot meant, but I couldn't keep my eyes focused. My lids kept drooping. The sun was so bright. The last thing I remembered—after a seemingly endless trek across an open plain—was the nasty gaseous mineral smells.

When I woke in my hammock I breathed in cautiously. The smell was not nearly so foul. I opened my eyes and saw beyond the treetops to a clear, dark sky. Even on this alien planet, I had my stars. I stroked Dot, who was wrapped around my neck like a stole. I turned my head and saw the sunset. Hadn't the sun been setting when I stumbled?

It wasn't the sun. It was a campfire at the edge of a scrubby forest. Two people, my mother and Gordy, were sitting near the open flame. She was teaching Gordy the words to a song.

"Old amber sparks and melts the juice.
The deep sea breathes,
Life blooms in salty water.
Cool, clear water.

It's time to sing for Mother Earth.
The deep sea breathes,
Each star's a pool of water.
Cool, Clear water."

While they were singing the vaguely familiar song, I drifted back to sleep.

Dot glowed with an incoming call. In my semi-dream state, I opened her to see the transmission.

"Virginia? Where are you?" a young man asked.

"I'm sleeping."

"The whole ship's turned inside out looking for you." It was Ray, standing in the navigation bay of the cruise ship. He whispered, "Your dad's a wild man."

"That's original information." I sat up and reoriented to my position on a hammock hanging in the wilderness of Green Tara. Zap.

Ray whispered, "I called to make sure you're safe."

I bristled at his concern. Ray was not my babysitter. The last time I'd seen him, he was knocked out in the main Navigation chair courtesy of my sleeping potion. I still felt a little guilty about that, and now I felt a little guilty for my sarcasm, especially when he seemed so sincere. "I'm fine. Just tired, and the smell out here . . . "

"Smell?"

I struggled to explain. "It's powerful. It's everywhere." How could I describe the strange smells of my planetary trek to someone who'd never been off ship? Plus, we were star systems apart.

"I'm worried about you," said Ray.

"Worried?" It was sweet that he would express concern. Still, I was suspicious. How had he found me? "Are you tracking me?"

"No," Ray said. "The instant messaging is courtesy of your dad. He invented a network that bounces signals off inter-planetary dust.

I nodded. I knew Dad had been developing a new communications technology, so that was no surprise.

He explained, "This call is one of the tests."

I still didn't understand why Ray had contacted me. Then Dad appeared behind Ray. "Virginia!"

"Dot! Dad's using you as a locator?"

"I did not initiate contact with your dad," Dot said, her eyes drifting behind the communicator view screen, like she was trying to hide from my anger. I still felt betrayed.

I leveled my next accusation toward Ray. "Traitor." This wasn't entirely fair, because he'd already said Dad had set up the call.

Ray shook his head, no, but I didn't want a further explanation from him.

And I absolutely did NOT want to talk to my dad. The last time I'd seen him, he had specifically told me NOT to follow my mom. I needed to figure out how to tell him that I'd disobeyed him in the extreme. Not only had I followed Momo's star chart—rescuing her in the process, a point that should go in my favor—but I'd flown off deck without a license, again—this time without a flight plan.

I slapped Dot's flap down.

"Ouch. Easy does it, girlfriend," Dot said from behind her plush cover. "A simple verbal command, 'end transmission,' would have worked just as well."

I snapped back, "Block that last caller."

Gordy must have seen I was awake. "Ginny," he waved me over to the campfire. "Look what Aunt Maureen found to eat."

My mother skewered a strange object with a straight stick and positioned it and two other loaded sticks over the fire. Spooky pranced between her and Gordy. He gave the kitten a small piece to nibble.

"I suppose anything's better than another F.R.E., but what is it?" I asked.

"I know. Tough to tell with so many body parts missing." My mother laughed and held up one of the oval-shaped bodies-on-a-stick. "They're cicadas." With her free hand she picked up a giant insect head and held it out for me to see. The lifeless red eyes, big as her fist, shone in the firelight.

"Scary." I clamped my own eyes shut.

"That's what I thought, too," she said. "But they don't move fast, or bite, or sting, so they're easy to catch. I used the legs and wings for kindling. The body has a fair amount of good meat, but the head's a little gooey." My mother tossed the head into the forest.

I opened my eyes just in time to see the head roll. "That's a real conversation stopper," I said, and she laughed. It felt great to make Momo laugh.

Everyone sat quietly gazing into the fire. Aside from the pop and crackle of green wood and insect body parts, the only other movement was when my mother turned the sticks to evenly grill the food. As it browned she lifted the roasting sticks away from the fire, cracked open the shells, and dropped the cooked food onto three large leaves.

Gordy took his leaf full and blew on it. As soon as it was cool enough he nibbled the meat. "It's salty."

"That's the skin, technically an outer membrane. If you don't like it, peel it off. The rest is quite mild."

Gordy licked his lips. He must have liked the taste because he popped a bigger chunk in his mouth. I nibbled around the edges of the meat. I wasn't wild about it, but I was hungry enough to eat it anyway. I tossed the skin back into the fire where it sparkled dramatically.

Momo broke the silence, "I've been thinking about Leo."

I wondered if she had received her own transmission from Dad.

Momo stared into the fire. "For me, so little time has passed, but Leo must have been very lonely."

I inhaled sharply and choked.

In between chews, Gordy said, "If you mean, did he find another woman? Don't worry. His heart still belongs to you. Isn't that right, Gin?" He whispered to me "Are you alright?"

I nodded while I gagged.

My mother spoke wistfully. "You may only see him as a father and uncle, but you should know about his loyalty and heroism. He's incredibly courageous."

My dad? Courageous? Hardly. A hero? "Ha," I laughed, except no sound came out. Instead, a swollen wad of meat slipped further down my throat.

"And he is the most exceptional inventor in generations." My mother sighed and voiced a confession. "I miss him."

I would have said, "Please, no over sharing of romantic sentiment." But I couldn't talk.

About this time Gordy must have realized that I wasn't breathing. He whacked me on the back. "Aunt Maureen!"

My mother jumped up, grabbed me from behind and, with a less than gentle squeeze around the middle, jerked me up in the air. A piece of cicada meat flew into the woods, and together we fell back onto the ground, gasping for breath.

⊕

Top of the Mountain

It took two long days to hike up the mountain. The entire climb I trailed behind Gordy. My mother was, of course, ahead of him. This order was the new normal.

As we rose higher in altitude there were fewer and fewer trees, and finally all that we passed on our way up were a few shrubs and flowers among the rocks. Even though we'd lost the shade and the grade was steep, it was cooler, pleasant even.

When I finally caught up with Gordy, he helped me up onto a rock and pointed back the way we'd come. I could see everything, the mountain forest below, the geyser field where I'd fainted, and the old growth woods in the distance that marked the location of Omega II.

We climbed over more boulders at the crest of the mountain and joined Momo. Here, looking in the other direction, the way we were going, the view was even more magnificent. A soft white blanket of clouds stretched from our feet to the western horizon.

No one said anything for the longest time. The clouds thinned and then parted, revealing the vast ocean below.

"Wow." I thought if anything could be truly breathtaking, this was it. The constantly moving light on water was dazzling.

Gordy shouted, "We made it!" and he started to trot down the mountain trail. "It's all downhill from here."

I hung back, still enchanted by the reflections on the water. My mother spoke gently, "It won't take nearly as long to climb down."

"It didn't look like this when we flew over the ocean. This color is so intense." I searched for a way to describe the blue that charged my eyeballs.

Momo smiled at me and nodded. "The quality and angle of the light and the level of the tide all affect the hue and intensity."

I took a deep belly breath. We'd left behind the pungent blend of forest smells and, up this high, all I took in through my nostrils was light. I suppose the best word for mountain top air is *pure*.

"Gin, I hope you think it's been worth the walk." Momo sat on a rock and offered me a handful of small, dark pieces of fruit. "Look what I found on the way up. Fresh blackberries." I took one purple berry and examined the surface. It had a multitude of shiny globes, all tightly bound into an oval-shape about the size of the end of my thumb. Momo popped one into her mouth.

I followed her lead and tested the berry with the tip of my tongue. I sucked it in and the flavor burst in my mouth. It was sweet and tangy, unlike any food I'd ever had in my entire life. I licked my lips and smiled. We ate all she'd picked, and her lips turned purple from the berry juice. I imagined mine had, too.

I took another deep breath and said, "It's stunning. And I'm glad we made it this far. But I wish ... " I couldn't quite identify what still felt missing.

"You wish what?" Momo asked.

Without knowing what I really had to say to her, I blurted, "You've always put this natural world stuff first. Your work, capital "W" – your research and your mission. But when I was growing up, I just ... I wish you'd been there."

She looked into the distance. When she responded I couldn't tell if she was being wistful or sarcastic. "You wish I'd combed your hair and kissed every scraped knee? That would have been a storybook childhood."

"No, I didn't want you around for just the stupid stuff. I wanted to know that I was important. You know—loved."

"You were and are loved, Gin. Without a doubt." Then her voice cracked. "I didn't want it to be this way. That's why Leo stayed behind. Even when I was gone, you had your father. And Dot. She's taken good care of you."

I rubbed my cheek against Dot's soft side and shut my eyes to hold back the tears.

"Gin. Gin." She whispered, "You haven't suffered. I'm the one who missed out. I missed all the wonderful moments you call *the stupid stuff*. The little things aren't stupid. I missed you growing up."

"Yeah, you missed all my childhood adventures," I whined.

"That's true," she said. "But what could be better than this glorious adventure? Look where we are now, Gin—Look." She pointed toward the ocean.

I stood up. The clouds streamed in, skirting the mountain again. White lay beneath our feet, with patches of ocean still visible in the distance. Momo and I stood on top of the world. She said, "We're together now."

It was fantastic, no argument. The setting, the adventure, getting to be a part of something with my Momo. But—I always had a *but*.

"Momo, I still don't understand how ...?"

"Gin, I don't have all the answers. But our mission is clear. Vera gave it her best effort, as did her daughter, and her daughter's daughter, and so on."

I looked at Momo and there was no denying our connection. "So, now it's you and me," I whispered. I'd been afraid to put Momo and me together—out loud—making us an *us*. The conclusion tumbled out. "Now, it's our turn."

"Now it's our turn," she nodded. "Who else but a Bosque woman could have read the star chart and followed it to Tara? I did it, and you did, too. Virginia, you faced formidable opposition to get this far. You saw past the misinformation and braved the Forbidden Zone. You are so capable. I'm so proud of you."

She kissed me on the forehead and turned to walk down toward the ocean.

I hesitated. We'd had our BIG TALK, and I was thrilled at the possibilities. I was on a real mission, together with Momo. But, my point—that we were putting too much effort into a lost cause—was left hanging. Momo had said she didn't have all the answers, and I held back wondering how to keep going on faith that together we could figure it all out.

Momo disappeared into the mist. It was tough for me to admit that she was right. We were finally together. Even though I couldn't see where she was going, for the moment I stopped repeating my *buts* and followed Momo into the cloud. For the moment I trusted that she and the trail would take us down the mountainside.

⊕

⊕

Low Tide at the Coast

It was early evening when we made it to the base of the mountain. Gordy ran all the way to the shoreline, where white sand met emerald green water. He took off his shoes, rolled up his pant legs, and ran out on a spit of sand that stretched into the ocean. At the farthest point he sat on a rock outcropping perched slightly above the constantly moving water.

I walked with Momo to the water's edge, though the "edge" wasn't a fixed position. The water kept moving, mostly pulling away from us. Momo called it low tide. We took off our shoes and walked along the smooth, glistening surface. It looked solid, but every step creaked, and grains of sand stuck to the bottom of my feet.

The two dominant things about the ocean up close were the rhythmic roar of the waves and the smell of salt, which permeated everything. But the sound and smell didn't overwhelm me in a negative way. Instead they made me feel peaceful.

Momo stopped where dark iron ore poked through the sand. She used the rock like a bench, and set her pack and herself down. She opened her tunic, and I saw she was wearing an amber pendant just like mine. She pulled the pendant over her head and tucked it safely into a waterproof pouch of her pack.

Over the sound of the moving tide, I heard mysterious whistles. I looked out where Gordy was surrounded by brilliantly colored birds. While Momo unloaded her gear, I waded closer to him, and I could hear him singing a song I recognized. The strangest thing was, it sounded like the birds were whistling along with him in perfect harmony, as he led them in a chorus of "Clear Water."

I paused, part way out on the sandbar, thinking that I might startle the birds and scare them away if I got too close. I opened Dot's face. "Look. It's a bird choir. I didn't know birds sang with humans."

Dot said, "Those birds appear to be related to the parrot, a species known for their bright plumage, vocal facility, and their ability to relate with humans."

"You recognize them?" I asked.

"Not exactly," she said. "Historically, a parrot's tendency is to bond with a mate and to defend its territory. They aren't known to be social in groups."

"You're saying they look like parrots, but don't act like parrots." Dot and I watched the singing flock. Occasionally one of the birds would break away from the swaying choir, dive into the water, and return to the surface with a fish in its beak.

"Their group dynamic and their fishing abilities are similar to the penguin species. Interesting." Dot pulled up pictures of both parrot and penguin so I could compare them to the flock of birds in this cove.

"Perhaps the two have interbred here on Tara," I said.

"That's unlikely, given the very specific mating behaviors of the two different species. It's possible we're seeing an accident in the terraforming process."

"Accidental species confusion?"

"In transit, it is possible that two egg types fused, mixing the genetic materials into new combinations, and when they were thawed and hatched here in the incubation tanks …"

I completed Dot's hypothesis, "… the parrots and penguins reconstituted into a new species."

"It may be premature to claim discovery of an entirely new species, based on casual observation," Dot said. "However, we are the only scientists within the Tara star system, and it is reasonable for us to make an interim assessment. Would you like to name our proposed new species?"

"Parrots and penguins. Paraguins, of course. Let's tell Momo." I waded back to shore and announced our discovery of the paraguin. Momo seemed fascinated with Dot's theory of fused eggs mixing the genes and wholeheartedly approved our new name.

Spread out on the rock I recognized a row of transparent mini cryo tubes. I asked, "You're planning to freeze the phytoplankton?"

"We need to keep the living plant viable," Momo said. "It's impossible to know how long it will take us to complete the mission."

"We're already going on seven generations," I said, stating the obvious.

"Seven's a lucky number." Momo responded as if the magnitude of seven generations was not an issue. She slipped each of the four tubes into a harness with a carrying strap. "I'm preparing one for each of us to carry, in case we get separated, and one extra, for safety."

Holding the tubes by their straps, she waded out past Gordy's point and allowed the tubes to float open, collecting the natural flora of the ocean. I admired her determination, even though I thought her plan was an impossible dream.

I walked the length of the sand bar and joined Gordy and the singing paraguins. I spread Dot's screen out on the sand, so Gordy could see her, too. "Dottie, explain again how the phytoplankton work."

Dot pulled up a page that she had scanned from the manuscript. "Hmm. A simple organism. Ooooh. This is interesting. Green Tara is the name of an ancient goddess whose domain was the protection of nature, especially all things living."

"This planet is named after a goddess?" Gordy snorted.

"Yes," Dot replied in her no-nonsense-stop-mocking tone. "*And* the phytoplankton in question is sometimes referred to as the "Greens of Tara."

"I sense a connection here." I held up my amber pendant and examined the algae inside of it. It was Dot's brain and, apparently, a precious fossil. "Tell us, oh wise one, how did algae get to be so important?"

"The Greens of Tara—we're talking phytoplankton—support life as we know it. They convert carbon dioxide to oxygen. You might say, it's their hobby." Dot chuckled at her own joke. "In addition to this most basic function, the greens are credited with the ability to eat industrial pollutants—though that's not an issue on this planet—and reduce them to harmless molecules"

I said, "And around your main brain is wrapped a genetic match."

"A perfect match," Dot said.

No matter how I looked at it, this was a bizarre connection. "So, you've got a simple organism on your massively complex processor."

"There's a lot going on in one space," Dot verified. "Just as the greens themselves carry companion bacteria that neutralize organic toxins."

"Why didn't the phytoplankton make oxygen on Earth? Why didn't they work in Great-gran Vera's time?" Gordy asked.

"Excellent question, Gordy. Phytoplankton and their microscopic cousins were plentiful in the oceans of Earth. But several factors compromised their ability to function. For one, the temperature of the surface waters rose, and it was simply too hot for these particular phytoplankton. These and their cousins were struggling to survive," Dot said.

"All because in the Age of Squandered Wealth people trashed the planet," I said.

"That was certainly a contributing factor, but to be fair, the final collapse came when a catastrophic volcanic explosion covered one continent in ash. That created unseasonably long winter conditions worldwide," Dot said.

"Life on Earth became unsustainable, and that's what motivated the colonists," I said, repeating what everyone knows about the ongoing search for habitable planets.

"There's more," said Dot. "The volcanic eruption was a disaster that many species could have survived in the long run. The first generation of colonists thought humans would be able to return to Earth once the ash had settled. Of course, we know it didn't work out that way."

"So what happened to completely kill off the oceans?" Gordy asked.

"This scientific information has been suppressed for generations," Dot said.

"Suppressed . . . by whom?" As soon as I asked, I realized it had to be the Triumvirate. The corporation controlled everything, even the flow of information. That's why our Great-gran Vera had hand-written her manuscript. Dot was an independent information source, too. I pressed her for the facts. "What really happened?"

"The initial volcanic explosion set off a chain of worldwide ruptures in the Earth's crust and thousands of man-made CO_2 storage beds split open. The massive volume of carbon dioxide released in such a short span of time created an acidic condition that killed all plant life on the surface," Dot said. "On land only a few hardy seeds of terrestrial shrubs survived. On the water—well, you know what happened to the phytoplankton."

"They didn't survive." I repeated what every schoolchild learns, "And without the primary oxygen generators, the entire planetary ecosystem collapsed."

The paraguins, humming soft and low, gathered around us. The birds, as if they were listening to our story, swayed together. Here was an entire species that had never known the old planet, yet they seemed to be in mourning. This may sound harsh, but honestly I didn't share any feeling of loss. Earth was nothing more than a cautionary history lesson to me.

Meanwhile, Momo floated in the center of the cove. She looked contented. She'd finally gotten her precious samples of phytoplankton, the key ingredient to fulfilling the Bosque mission.

I still struggled with the pressure of inheriting Great-gran Vera's plan. Sure, it was heroic, but it was too late, and there were too many factors against us. I blurted my thoughts, "All we have is an illustrated story in a handwritten book. There's no research about how the greens could re-oxygenate a planet. There are too many variables."

"Consider this: Is there any record of how or why the Eyebright remedy might work?" Dot asked.

"Zero official scientific record," Gordy said. "But the plant healed Spooky's eyes."

"Correct. Or, using an ancient colloquial, your great-grannie was on to something," Dot said.

I was stymied. "Dot, you've always been the rational voice. Now you're acting all woo-woo and embrace-the-mystery, and I don't like it."

Gordy, obviously done with discussion time, chased Spooky across a tide pool and onto another sand bar.

I doodled in the sand while I absorbed the weight of the family mission. This was more than huge, more than any sane person would try to accomplish, not willingly. Restoring life to an entire planet? *I* wasn't capable of taking on this kind of responsibility. I grumbled, "This is different than Spooky's eyes. You can't heal what's already dead." But Gordy couldn't hear me, and Dot chose not to respond.

I stretched out and rested my head on Dot's soft form, watching the waves, feeling the ocean breathe. Feeling the energy. Remembering the water on this planet was full of life. The scale of it was unfathomable.

An iridescent creature appeared above me, hovering for a moment. Then it sped into an orbit around my head, finally parking just in front of my face and fixing his multifaceted eyes on mine. His coppery-ringed body was remarkably still, suspended in the air, while his two pairs of translucent wings beat so rapidly they were little more than a blur. He rose above my head again, staying close enough that I could still feel the whisper of his wings.

Another creature, his cousin, swung past in a blur to my right, and another approached behind my left ear. Soon, an entire flock hovered all around me and my hair floated up, electrified. I didn't say a word. I didn't want to disturb the moment. I was at once charged and relaxed, and for the first time on the expedition, I was comfortable with the sights, the sounds *and* the smells of the natural world around me. I was no longer an observer traveling *through* the wilderness. I had become part of the energetic life here. Then one by one the gentle creatures left my side to congregate on a nearby pool.

In a hushed tone I asked, "What are those?"

"Dragonflies," Dot said. "Very large dragonflies."

"I've never seen anything so beautiful," I said.

"Of course, I'm only speculating, but I think I can see why your great-grandparents Vera and George would risk everything to give these creatures a home." Dot looked at me with liquid eyes, "Gin Gin. Your ancestral planet has rested for many generations. Perhaps now the time is ripe."

I watched Gordy dive after a trio of frolicking paraguins. Apparently the birds were teaching him to swim. I contemplated what else we might learn from the creatures of Great-gran Vera's sanctuary. While Gordy and the paraguins played, I rocked to the tempo of the living ocean and felt the tide shift. The waves were starting to come back in to shore.

⊕

⊕

Paraguin Cove

The phytoplankton samples froze successfully. Given their simple structure, Momo believed they would thaw quickly and easily. So, our mission to the coast was a success.

We christened our favorite beach *Paraguin Cove* and made a delicious soup, flavored with salty seaweed. Though there were plenty of rocks along the coast, we saw none with a keyhole passageway. So, how our Great-gran Vera and George had come to Tara remained a mystery.

At low tide we followed the sand around the southern tip of Paraguin Cove and explored the remnants of Omega I. Most of it had been washed away by countless tides. The only evidence of the first terraforming efforts were a few metal racks made to hold egg hatching trays, crudely forged from Green Tara ore. An adjacent tide pool, filled with undulating sea urchins and skittering crabs, suggested the variety of life forms that had been spawned in this very location.

I wanted to sleep on the sandy beach, but Dot predicted a higher than usual tide overnight, so we began our trek back. Our uphill climb was painfully slow, but I didn't mind. It meant more time with the smell of salt in the air. At the tree line, I hung my hammock where I had an unobstructed view of the sunset over water. Before I saw the ocean it meant nothing to me. Now it felt like everything.

Gordy fell asleep quickly, curled up with Spooky. Momo was asleep, too, cradling the quartet of collection tubes. I wasn't sleepy though. Instead of feeling exhausted like I had on the first leg of our trek, I felt strangely light. Despite the facts—we were still stranded on a lost planet without the means to complete our mission—I felt peaceful and at the same time charged. Every pore on my body was open to the energy circulating around me and how it connected to the energy within.

A loon called in the distance. The sound made me smile. I breathed deeply, thankful that I was no longer afraid of Green Tara's night sounds. Two other birds, too small to be loons, tore through the treetops. Then all I could hear were the waves far below. I watched shooting stars spill into the ocean.

Suddenly my view was blocked by a large bird. It turned and glided gracefully inland. Overhead, it looked far larger than a loon. It was enormous.

Zap! The bird crashed into a high branch and tumbled down through limbs and leaves. It made a high-pitched squealing noise—maybe it was a bat—bounced off a lower branch and landed on one end of my hammock. I scrambled off. Simultaneously, Momo appeared by my side and bopped the flailing creature on the head. It crumpled upside down on the ground, one leg still tangled in the hammock rope. Momo said, "Get a light."

I focused Dot's high beam on the pile of ropes. It wasn't a bird or a bat. It was a full-grown human. From the groan, he sounded male. This was a stranger encounter than a giant bat would have been. The man hadn't just dropped from the stars, but where had he come from? I pulled away some of the ropes and what was left of a hang-gliding sail, exposing the man's unmistakable hair. "Dad?"

By this time Gordy was awake, too. "Uncle Leo?"

Dad grunted and wriggled. "You're both here." He rolled over and managed to raise his head, squinting in Dot's focused light. "Thank the stars I found you."

Momo hung back in the shadows while we untangled Dad's feet, and pulled the hang-gliding straps off his shoulders. "He's free now, Dot." She dimmed her light, so we could see each other, but not so blinding. And I pulled Dad to his feet.

Momo stepped forward. "You're Leo?"

He looked at Momo closely. "Mo!?"

She said, "You look so old."

⊕

Airlift to the String Machine

Nothing could have been stranger than seeing Dad airlift Momo from the mountainside up to Dad's silver jet. Through the leaves I saw him kiss her. Zap. Then they took off. And then Gordy and I waited for Dad to return, me on the ground and Gordy still up in the tree. He's such a monkey. I know because Dot showed me a picture of one. It had its long arms wrapped around a branch, and it looked just like him.

Gordy called down from the treetop, "I see Uncle Leo's String Machine. Get ready, Gin."

From the forest floor I couldn't see anything, so I swatted away annoying insects and waited for the airlift to take me out of the creepy-crawlie zone. Thank the stars we were finally done walking on the surface.

Since there wasn't a viable place to land on the mountainside, Dad had parked his String Machine in hover mode while he'd hang-glided down to our campsite the night before. Dot had nicknamed him "Batman" for his surprise landing on my hammock. In the morning, he'd devised a plan to drop an airlift caddy and one at a time bring us onboard and transport us inland, back to Omega II.

It hadn't taken long for him to drop off Momo. Especially, compared to the days it had taken us to walk the same distance. The caddy dropped down through the leaves. I buckled the straps around my waist and legs and yelled, "Hoist away!" and up I went.

I waved at Gordy on my way past him. He looked so comfortable hanging onto the high branch, guiding the airlift ropes. Above the tree canopy, I crawled into Dad's String Machine, loosened the harness straps and said, "Let's jet," thinking it would be another round trip before he would be back for Gordy. But Dad had done a weight calculation. Gordy and I and the balance of our gear were under the String Machine's weight limit. So Dad sent the air caddy down again for Gordy, and showed me how to operate the hoist system.

The whole airlift task went smoothly. Gordy leaned his long torso through the open cockpit, dropped Spooky in, and pulled himself inside. The cabin wasn't exactly spacious, though. I asked Dad, "Are you sure there's room?"

"I can handle it." Gordy wiggled back into the jump seat.

Leo helped him tuck his arms and legs into the small space. "Gordy! I do believe you're taller. Your voice has dropped, too."

Gordy shrugged. I hadn't noticed how much he'd changed during the short time we'd been on Green Tara.

I buckled myself into the co-pilot's seat. Of course, questions raced through my mind. The night before, our family conversation had centered on Momo's last memories of Tara before she had gone into the cryo tube. Typical Dad had reeled off a handful of highlights of our years onboard the colonial cruiser. Typical me wanted to know more. I still hadn't heard all the details about how he managed to take off from the cruise ship without raising Triumvirate alerts.

Dad finished storing the airlift gear and buckled himself into his pilot's seat.

Our next move was maneuvering up and over the peak, so I opened the navigation pane. I'd been in Dad's machine before, but I wanted to see how he'd adjusted flight settings for the atmosphere and gravitational variables.

"Virginia, I can see the planetary life hasn't harmed you one nano spot," Dad said.

"No visible scars. It's the overpowering smells that get to me," I said.

"Aunt Maureen says she looks and talks just like my mom," Gordy said.

"Celia?" Dad said. "Yes, I suppose she does." He looked at me and smiled. "She's beautiful, too."

I recognized a compliment—rare coming from Dad under any circumstances. It was especially nice to hear considering the last time I saw him I'd defied his explicit instructions to stay put.

Dad said, "I could jet to the lab in minutes, but let's take a more leisurely tour. Show me what I missed." He flew slowly enough that we could clearly see the surface. We followed the same path that we had walked, only in the sky and in reverse.

Gordy pointed to the steaming geyser field below. "That's where Virginia passed out from heat exhaustion." Of course, every sight reminded Gordy of the details of our trek, and he continued with non-stop narration for the entire flight.

I tuned out most of Gordy's account. My attention went to how different Dad looked out of the tight collar of a Triumvirate uniform. His hair was wild, and at the open neckline of his flight jacket I caught a glimpse of an amber pendant, like the ones Momo and I wore. Most of all, he was relaxed.

Spooky pranced back and forth across the dash—even that didn't bother Dad. It was like he had a completely different personality.

Even at our leisurely pace we made it to Omega II within an hour, and Dad set the String Machine down in the clearing near my Galaxy Blast.

He already had a plan for freeing the upside-down space coupe, and he set Gordy to work immediately.

While Gordy secured a towing harness onto the Blast, I finally had a chance to ask Dad a question, "What took you so long?"

"What took me so long?" he asked.

"I mean, once you figured out where we were, why didn't you come rescue us right away?"

"You know the Triumvirate protocol. I had to get the String Machine cleared for an unscheduled flight. My justification was to follow your kidnappers, the pirates." Dad smiled. "The Skats created the perfect diversion. You figured that out before I did."

"So when Ray contacted me, you already knew about Green Tara?"

"Don't blame the young man. He didn't know when I used his com line to contact you that it would make you angry. I didn't know you'd be so angry. But I needed to check in with you. I saw the Galaxy Blast on the manifest of stolen items. That was my clue you were in your pilot's seat. You're so much like your mother. And following the star chart to Tara! Ginny-the-Genius. That's you." He kissed me on the forehead and jumped out. "Come on, Gin."

Instead of basking in the praise, I focused on the fact that he hadn't satisfactorily answered my first question about why he'd taken so long to follow Gordy and me to Tara. That, on top of the other small issue—he had failed to even try to rescue Momo when she'd disappeared. I grumbled to myself, "Even on the backside of a lost planet he's too busy to finish a conversation with me."

I slid over the lip of the cockpit and landed on the springy planet surface, intent on pursuing my line of questioning, and—zap—my middle-aged father plucked a golden wildflower, bowed formally, and offered the gift to my mother. Ew. Ew. Ew.

Gordy cartwheeled past the courtship scene, as if it were no eyesore, and into the midst of a group of people. When had the population of Green Tara jumped from three—four counting my dad—to thirty-five? Was I hallucinating?

A woman welcomed Gordy and waved me over to a table where a dozen or so bowls of fruit and salad filled a long table. The fresh food looked delicious, and when a young girl waved I automatically waved back.

Wait. I recognized her.

The girl was one of the faces I remembered from the Llama 33, the exploration pod that the cruise ship dumped. It was as if I were watching a Dot video log from what felt like a lifetime ago—in reality only a couple of weeks—the day of my ill-fated test flight. Except, the colonists weren't crammed inside the pod. They were moving freely about.

I approached the gathering and saw the spherical pod parked in the shade on the other side of the clearing. A man picked up the girl I'd recognized and welcomed me. "Leo Bosque is your father, isn't he?" I nodded. "Then you already know how special he is."

As if on cue, Dad led Momo to my side, shook the man's hand, and introduced him to Momo. The man bowed his head and gushed, "I'm honored to meet you." Then he set the little girl down and knelt beside her, telling her my mother was the famous scientist and explorer. They were looking up at Momo like she was a goddess. Meanwhile, a speechless woman approached Dad and clung to him, bawling. It was embarrassing, watching grown-ups display their emotions, and I stepped back.

More people crowded around Dad and Momo.

The girl ran around in circles. "Zip, ziparee! Mr. Bosque set us free. He towed us here, to the promised land."

I decided I wasn't hallucinating. Too much detail for that. And I finally put it together. This is what had taken Dad so long. Before he flew to Tara to find us, me and Gordy and Momo, he rescued the drifting Llama 33 and brought the colonists to Tara.

True: I had personally fallen in love with dragonflies, paraguin song, and salty ocean spray. But, these people were calling Tara—an insect-infested, sulfur-spewing planet—the *promised land.*

And my dad, the one who never wanted to take a risk or in any way defy Triumvirate rules, was their hero.

⊕

Communication Gaps

I've always known Dad was a brilliant inventor. But a true hero? This was new information. And Momo? She had her own reputation as a scientist and resistance leader. So my recent discoveries about her true nature, the courageous woman willing to risk her life to set the world right, and Dad's rescue of the otherwise doomed pod of colonists, put me in the last-to-know category. Two fabulous parents. No argument there.

But the two of them together? Allow me to make an observation: They weren't the smoothest team in the galaxy. They argued over ridiculous, minor points. Not about what to do next, but about how to explain what they wanted to do. "If you'd said this. If you'd said that." I don't know how they manage to get anything done. On the communication front, I resented the fact that neither one of them told me anything, except when one of them decided it was time for me to follow direct orders. My cynical self wondered if the conflict between them was the real reason Dad never went on a search and rescue mission for Momo.

Despite all the conflict, somehow, together they'd engineered an elegant way to fly the space coupes in tandem. The idea was to marry the assets of the two different engines into one incredibly fast and flexible craft. Also, they planned larger living quarters between my scramjet and Dad's custom ship, so the four of us would have more room for our long, interstellar flight. It was still going to be a tight fit, and imagining us as a cozy, happy family was … unimaginable.

Dad positioned his silver String Machine parallel to my stranded Blast and he and Gordy connected the two with struts he'd found in the building supplies of the research lab. Sounds complicated, but that part didn't take long. By late afternoon our Bosque family space ship looked something like a pontoon boat slung upside-down in the branches of the cypress tree. Now we needed to flip the whole thing over.

Dot and I managed to free the Blast's back hatch. Turned out there was no physical block or damage, so getting inside was easy.

On top of the parental communication problems, and my general uncertainty about everything, maneuvering the coupes in tandem was going to be the real test. Everyone was tense as Dad got into his pilot's seat with Momo as co-pilot, and I sat in the Blast cockpit with Gordy by my side.

Dad spoke over the com-line, "Buckle up, kids."

We were sitting upside down, and the gravity of the planet was in full force. We couldn't *not be buckled* up and stay in our seats. I mocked, "Buckle up, kids." Thanks a lot, Dad. Every move required conscious effort. I pulled my headset down—actually up, with respect to gravity—

and said into it, "Ready." I reached over the console where Dot was positioned to pin her face flap open, but as soon as I took my hands off my mouthpiece it dropped down away from my chin. This was incredibly awkward, and I wished we could have gotten the Blast out first and then tied the two ships together. But the way it had landed in the branches, I couldn't use any of my jet engines without damaging the tree.

"We're going to take this in 90-degree stages. First I'll pull us up with the String Machine side," Dad said. "Stay prepared with a cushion from your crest thrusters, but fire them *only* if we become unstable."

"When we become unstable," I grumbled more to myself than anyone. It wasn't something I was announcing on the com line. I was just venting. I hate it when he tells me everything to do that I obviously already know.

The power grid hummed and Dad said, "Remember Gin-Gin, this could be a little bumpy, so don't bite your tongue."

"Remember Gin-Gin," I mocked Dad again, "Don't bite your tongue."

"That's harsh." Gordy said, "He's doing the best he can."

"If he was doing his 'best' he would have taken care of Momo a long time ago, and we wouldn't be . . . AH." Our tandem ship surged and then dropped back with a thump. "Ow." I bit my tongue.

Dot chimed in, "Your father did not rescue your mother when she 'disappeared' because he had strict instructions not to travel here. It was too risky. The wrong forces would have followed him and destroyed everything, including your mom."

"How do you know?" I snapped at Dot.

"Dot knows everything," Gordy said.

"Whose side are you on?" I snapped at Gordy.

"I'm quoting you," he said, deadpan.

Before I could think of a decent comeback, the ship surged again and slowly pivoted upward and stopped. The ships' noses pointed straight up, and everything that wasn't locked into place shifted, my clothes, my hair, my mouthpiece.

Dad said, "I'm going to examine our position. Gordy, meet me outside." Gordy slid out of his seat and out the back hatch, and Dad did the same on the String Machine side.

Everyone else seemed so eager and happy. Momo waved to me from the other cockpit.

On the opposite end of the spectrum, I felt trapped. Physically stuck with my back pressed into the pilot's seat, my brain latched onto my last clear thought—admittedly a harsh thought. I hissed through clenched teeth, "Why didn't anyone tell me Momo was here. We had ten years to rescue her!"

"Virginia," Dot said patiently. "Not long after your mother was officially considered 'missing' your cruise ship left the sector. This planet has been out of range."

"Oh device of all knowledge, if he couldn't make it across the sectors, how in the stars are we supposed to make it back to Earth in this rinky-dink vessel?"

"Leo's been perfecting much-much-faster-than-light technology and specifically the String Machine for—ahem—guess how many years?" Dot raised her eyebrows.

I squirmed in my seat. "Ten."

"Leo's String Machine can hitch a ride on the fastest energy strands in the galaxy. And it gets better," Dot said. "Theoretically, the total system design of our tandem coupes exponentially enhances operating capacity. He's designing viable interstellar space travel, even as we speak."

"So now I'm supposed to feel guilty for hating him, when all my life he's been trying so hard," I said.

"I would never recommend wallowing in guilt. That's an unwise use of human energy," Dot said. "Furthermore, I don't believe you actually hate your dad."

Dot was right, as always. Saying "hate" and feeling capital-H *Hate* were not the same. Not even close.

I glanced outside. Gordy was chasing Spooky across the grass, and Momo was on the ground arguing with Dad. I leaned out my window and said to them, "I thought we were supposed to stay in our seats."

My cockpit was hanging out in mid-air, so I slid out the back hatch onto the cypress limb. We'd definitely made progress. The Blast was now freed from the tree and suspended in the tandem craft structure. From what I could tell, Dad wanted to leave the ship in its 90-degree position, but Momo didn't.

"Moving them again would waste energy," Dad said. "We'll want the boost when it's time to leave orbit." He noticed me hanging over them and said, "Careful, sweetheart. I still haven't solidly connected your Blast to the frame. Once we're ready to blow the exoskeletal shell in place it'll be solid." He patted the ship's frame.

"How in the stars can we build the living quarters like this?" Momo said.

"I'll design a gyro platform," Dad said.

"That'll cause other problems," she said, "More delays."

"There're always integration problems. Nothing insurmountable," he said.

"You just want to spend your life designing perfection. We don't need perfect, we need good enough."

"Mo." Dad reached for Momo's shoulder, trying to diffuse her frustration. She shook him off.

I called, "Dad, she's right. Forget perfection."

Momo looked up at me, "And you. I heard what you said. How dare you question your father's motives or loyalty?" Her voice had that *you've crossed the line* tone.

Zap. I'd left the com line open and she'd overheard my conversation with Dot about Dad taking so long to rescue her.

Dad said "This hasn't been easy for any of us, Maureen." He didn't say anything to me. He just looked at me with those sad, disappointed eyes.

"Your father and I took on this mission willingly, together. We knew the risks. And we didn't do—or not do—things to please you or punish you."

That stung.

⊕

⊕

Avoiding Family Contact

I was confused. When Dad was stuck in his can't-take-action mentality, I sided with Momo, but she sided with him and said I was disloyal. Zap.

Within days Dad had the gyro platform working perfectly, so our living quarters would maintain a stable orientation whatever our tandem ship's course or pitch. In the long run his design feature would make for a more flexible and far more comfortable ride. So, I grudgingly admitted, if only to myself, that he hadn't been stalling and indecisive, after all. I wondered if Momo had come to the same conclusion.

But I didn't ask because I was completely avoiding conversation with her—easy enough to do, since she and I had failed in the art of intimate *tête-à-têtes*—and instead kept myself busy with the colonists and their education in planetary life. Dot and I taught them everything we knew about bird propagation. It wasn't much, because everything I knew came from the one mini-lesson Momo had given in the aviary before we started on our trek. Basically, any eggs not used for food, would grow into the next generation of birds. Dot pulled some research on high-yield egg production in domesticated birds, in other words, how to get enough eggs so there would be plenty for humans to eat. Her advice was to make the birds comfortable.

While we constructed an airy room for them with rows of nesting boxes on every side, each lined with dried grasses, Dot crowed and cackled and honked. She said she was making the birds feel welcome. I suspect she was adding to her audio files for later playback. Meanwhile, I noticed that individual birds had specific preferences, but generally, the ducks liked their nests low to the ground, and the chickens seem to feel safer, waist high.

While I developed expertise in domestic egg production, Gordy worked for and played around everyone, equally at home with our family and the colonists. I envied his good-natured temperament.

Meanwhile, Momo was busy with her own vision of our future. She recruited some of the colonists to transplant trees from the planet surface to inside the central chamber of our ship. She wanted trees large enough to hang our hammocks upon. A more obvious choice, certainly simpler, would have been to build frames with scrap construction materials. I didn't speak to her personally, but I did make the observation—in passing to anyone who might be listening—that I thought her idea of trees inside our living quarters was a ridiculous waste of space. Momo shrugged off my comment and said the trees were more than hammock support. They would provide oxygen during our voyage.

Once the root system of the trees was securely in place and the flooring was installed above the soil, Momo gathered the family together in our new living quarters. As the others convened I walked through and explored what would be our home. The effect of the trees was the opposite of what I'd feared. Instead of feeling crowded, the great room, with its interesting divisions and variety of spaces, felt larger than it had when it was bare.

Momo had the four of us stand in a circle. I thought she'd brought us together to celebrate the completion of one phase of construction, but I realized what we were actually marking was the beginning of the next phase of our journey. This ceremony was about the future.

She handed us each a necklace made with a vial of phytoplankton. She called Gordy and me the seventh generation and said it was our task to fulfill the Bosque destiny. If she'd told us to hold hands, or if she'd talked on and on about greater importance or the humans who were counting on us to make the Earth right again, I might have barfed. But she kept it simple and when I put my necklace on, I felt a powerful bond with my family. Some of the rough edges melted away, and our mission felt less like an impossible dream and more like what we were meant to do.

We had lunch together and shared Green Tara's best fresh food. And afterwards, when everyone else left the structure to focus on another task, I stayed to hang the hammocks. When they were up, I climbed into mine and lingered, looking up into the canopy of leaves we were taking with us. After two weeks on Green Tara it was hard to imagine space flight again. Our journey would be so different from living on the colonial cruise ship and different than short trips flying my tiny Blast solo. It was unclear how long we'd be on our ship.

Dad was planning a clear outer shell for our family ship, so there was going to be plenty of star viewing on our interstellar trip. I liked that. It was lovely, all of it, and I was glad we were taking something of Green Tara with us.

I poked my head outside and waved to Gordy. He was crouched on a tree limb—one that would stay on the planet—just under the central gyro support structure with Spooky draped across his shoulders. I climbed out and saw that he was painting a sign on the ship's hull. The new name was *The Tree House*.

"Perfect." I smiled. "Come on, Gordy. Check out our new sleeping quarters."

"I've seen it."

"I know you've been inside. I hung the hammocks."

Gordy stood up and teased Spooky's whiskers. "I want to sleep one more night in the wilderness."

"We're bringing the wilderness with us." I walked along the enormous tree branch and leaned against the sturdy trunk. I felt the ridges of the bark press a pattern into my skin. "I had Dot record bird song and insect buzz."

Gordy shut his eyes. "Does Dot do smells?" Spooky leapt off and skittered out the branch. Gordy crawled after him.

Despite my own aversion to most wilderness smells, I asked, "Dot, what can you do for Gordy that won't make me puke?"

But, before Dot replied I heard a strange, yet familiar giggle. My first thought was it was a bird call and, if only I could remember, I would have returned the call.

⊕

Trapped Under The Tree House

From the massive branch of the old cypress, I heard the familiar giggle again. This time the bird call was very close, coming from below, and I no longer thought it was a bird.

I looked down on a tall, skinny pirate. He'd been on the colonial ship. He must have sensed me, because he looked up and we locked eyes. Our sparsely occupied planet had just gotten a little too crowded. He giggled again and threw a net up, trapping me in a magnetic hold. My previous personal encounters with pirates had gone pretty well. But, this time, I couldn't move.

"Gotcha!" He pulled me easily to the ground and slipped a lock on the net. "Lookee at the girlee," he called out gleefully and ran off.

I couldn't turn my head to see where the skinny fellow went. Zap! I couldn't move at all. I could see my parents, though, trapped in their own net on the other side of the tree where they had been working only moments before. I looked for Gordy. He'd just been up in the tree with Spooky and me. Maybe the pirate hadn't seen him, yet.

The one skinny pirate reappeared with a gang of four more. This was the same gang Gordy and I had seen from behind a stack of synth straw just outside Impound. How had this they found us on Tara? The pirates circled and eyed my parents and me, then left the shade and swaggered toward Omega II. My guess was our family didn't have anything in hand worth looting, so they'd moved on.

Then I saw Gordy out of the corner of my eye. He was shimmying along the tree branch above. I told Dot, "Thank the stars. Gordy will get us out of this." I hoped he had his demagnetizer—the one he used to destabilize SensEyes. But instead of pulling out his little gun, he pointed toward the clearing, and I saw what he saw. It was the entire band of Skats!

Thirty or more pirates swarmed around Omega II, raiding equipment, plants, anything and everything they could carry away from the research lab. "Dot," I cried, though she was just as trapped as I was.

She said, "Remember, Skats are known to value a fair trade."

"They're not here to trade. What they're doing is called stealing." I closed her face flap. "Now be quiet."

I wondered what would happen to the colonists. Most of them were working on their new outpost. I knew some were in their land rover scouting the nearby terrain. They were capable, but no match for a band of Skats. It was only a matter of time before they were captured, too.

The twins, Lora and Lee, crossed the clearing and pulled the net off my head. My first reaction was relief. "I'm so glad you know we're not hardcore Triumvirate."

Lora said, "Trivert or not . . ."

". . . you threw power bolts at our ship," Lee said.

"We're here for revenge." Lora disabled the lock on my net, and then pointed to our new family ship, the Tree House. "And a prize."

Lee looked up and clapped. "I want a tree house."

I protested, "You can't strip down our ship, too. You'll leave us stranded."

Lora said, "No, we won't."

Lee said, "We'll take you with us."

No. There was a lot to like about these girls, but I wasn't ready to join up with them. Even if I wanted to, my family and I had other plans. And I doubted our effort to restore life on a long-dead planet would fall in the Skat's trajectory.

Lora seemed to know what I was thinking. "Being a Skat isn't so bad."

"You're already an outlaw," Lee said

"With us, you'll have sisterhood."

"And a life traveling the stars." The twins linked arms with me and did a little dance. For a sweet moment I was tempted by their carefree life.

We spun to an abrupt stop, and a big man loomed over us.

"Very Perry," said Lora, bowing.

"Genuine Gin Bosque," said Lee, introducing me.

Perry, the infamous leader of the Skats, growled at me. "Lost a pair of gyros chasing you at the Zone edge."

"I didn't intend any damage." And I thought back to the time Dot threw bolts at the Skats so that they wouldn't follow us to Tara. Obviously, our escape had been temporary.

He snarled. "Your shot-across-the-bows escape trick blew my balance beams."

"That sounds inconvenient. Again, my apologies." I had no idea what kind of revenge he had in mind. Dad had said the Skats were notorious for their unpredictable behavior.

"Perry. Perry ..." Lora said.

"... Very merry ..." Lee said.

"... We think ..." Lora said.

"... this one's got the spirit ..." Lee said.

"... to make a copper-bottomed Skat," Lora said.

"She can charge a hull, for sure. Figured that out without proper training." Perry circled me, looking me over, head to toe. Finally, he stopped and whistled long and low. "Recruit her."

Wow. I was surprised when two teenage girls wanted me to join them. But I could never have anticipated this offer from the head of a band of pirates. I said, "It's tempting. But what about them?" I pointed to my parents.

"The net's not as strong as a cryo freeze," Lee said.

"But it'll suppress their appetites," Lora said.

"Long enough to last," Lee said.

"Till more Triverts get here," Lora said.

"More Triverts?"

"He's a wanted man," Lee said.

"So's she," Lora said.

"No," I protested, grabbing Perry's arm. "Let them loose!"

"What's in it for me?" Perry asked, sarcastically.

"We've got something of value to trade," I blurted. I wasn't sure what I could offer that he would want, but I knew Skats loved to bargain.

"Your ship toy?" Perry sneered.

No! Not our ship. I needed to offer the Skats something of real value. Zap. I could trade the one basic thing that every traveler needs: *Water.* "We have a water generator," I said in a rush. And to underline the real value, I took a deep breath and lowered my voice. "Free powered."

"Free powered?" Perry asked.

"With enough capacity for your entire crew," I said. "It's simple to use. My dad designed it, and he's the best inventor in the galaxy."

"Free water." Perry seemed interested.

"My mother will convince him that outfitting you is the right move."

Perry shook his head. "Undercover mentality." His body language told me he didn't trust my mother.

I tried to relate my family and my trade offer to something he would feel strongly about. "My parents' mentality is that of the water bearer," I said, referring to the Skats' home, deep in the Constellation Aquarius.

"What's Aquarius to you?" Perry sounded suspicious. Generations ago the Skat clan had been the first to break from Triumvirate rule, and they still maintained a largely unseen presence among the outposts.

"Water is the source of life." I underlined the practical benefit of a short-term allegiance. "The water we can give you is priceless."

"Only if you share as a comrade," Perry said.

"Only if it's all of us," I said.

"I'm not fighting the oldsters to get you. He's a Trivert drone," he said.

"He's not a loyalist. He's been working for the Earth Restoration Alliance."

"An agent for the E.R.A.?" Perry chuckled. "She's a rebel gone solo act. Too hard to integrate with our collective spirit."

"My mother's not a solo act. We're a family."

"What kind of family?" He put his arms softly around the twins' shoulders. "I'd never leave these girls behind. Raised them from pups." Perry looked at my mother. "I hear she left you knee high."

"How do you know that?" It was creepy that he knew personal information about me.

"The Bosque sisters are legendary," Perry said in a mocking tone of voice.

When Perry talked about the Bosque *sisters*, he could only mean my mom and Gordy's. I risked a quick glance up, and sure enough Gordy looked like he was ready to drop out of the tree and strangle the man. I shook my head, hoping the pirates wouldn't realize I was communicating with him and not just protesting the insult to my family. As long as they didn't know about Gordy, he had a chance to escape. Gordy held his breath and kept silent.

"No promise." Perry instructed the twins, "Leave the old ones in the net. You keep the girl."

The twins gleefully pranced to my sides, locked arms with me again, and spun me in a circle. Round and round we went, as the twins led me toward the Skat space ship.

I was crushed. I thought I'd made an excellent trade offer, but I hadn't convinced the Skat leader that we could be allies. I was in the pirates' custody, and my parents were locked in a trap.

⊕

Joy Ride with the Twins

I'd never had close girl friends on the cruiser, but if I'd known Lora and Lee growing up, I had a feeling that we would have been an inseparable trio. The twins spent the rest of the afternoon adding color to my eyelids and dressing me up in a pair of bright argyle pantaloons. I had so much fun that for a while I forgot they were my captors. I did remember, however, to keep Dot wrapped up so they couldn't see her unique features. No point in tempting thieves, even friendly thieves.

That evening, the Skats built a fire outside and roasted vegetables they had confiscated from the colonists. The cook was fretting about not having meat on his menu, so I led him to a nearby tree where cicadas were clinging to the trunk and told him how to prepare the giant insects. He was delighted. Later, he was still grinning when he offered me a chunk with my vegetables, but I passed on the meat.

I sat between Lora and Lee on the outer ring of the campfire circle. The Skats didn't seem nearly as scary in this setting. They were friendly. Someone started to play music on a stringed instrument. Then, in the flickering firelight I saw that all the colonists were caged now, and that reminded me my parents were trapped and my eyes got hot. I covered my face with Dot, pretending there was nothing to hide. But Lora and Lee seemed to know my mood.

"Come on Gin Ginny."
"Don't look so glum."
"Bust off your beam ends."
"Let's have some fun."
"An escapade!"

The girls each grabbed an arm, stood me up and pranced me around in a silly, spontaneous jig.

A fun escapade? That gave me an idea. "How would you like to go for a ride?"

The twins squealed. "Oh, yes!"

"Shh," I said. And I motioned them to follow me into the night. I finally had a plan, admittedly vague, to rescue my family.

If the other Skats hadn't been drinking spirits and too inebriated to notice movement in the night, or if the campfire hadn't been on the far side of the research lab from the Tree House, I would never have been able to take the twins on a moonlight ride. But we made it to the Blast undetected.

Lora and Lee managed to keep quiet until we'd climbed into the cockpit. Inside they squealed with delight and explored every little corner, including every article of survival gear in the bottom of the storage bin. I rolled Dot out onto the navigation console, shushing her before she chimed in with a typical wisecrack. I still wanted to conceal her full capabilities. Dot winked an acknowledgement and shut her eyes before the twins caught a glimpse of the expressive nature of her screen side.

My Blast was still coupled with the family tandem ship, but Dad hadn't yet blown the exoskeleton, so all I had to do was unbolt the Blast from the larger framework. Then I got the twins seated in the co-pilot's seat, Lora on Lee's lap, and I flew my quiet ion-powered ship straight up and above the tree canopy. I headed west with the hope that, if the pirate twins saw the ocean and if I explained the importance of restoring life on Earth, they would understand why it was so important to free my family and allow us to complete our mission.

The ocean sparkled in the moonlight. Skimming above the water in the cove where Gordy and I sang with the paraguins, I flew southward along the coast, and tried to explain what the movement of the waves felt like. But Lora and Lee didn't seem at all interested. They'd never seen an ocean the way I had, up close and personal. They'd never had the chance to body surf. So I thought if I could find somewhere to land on the beach, they could experience the toes in-the-sand effect for themselves. I searched the shoreline for a good spot.

Lee started to complain about feeling crushed. She was on the bottom. Lora said, "Let's flip," and she got up to change places.

When Lee crawled on top of Lora, somehow she knocked the scramjet's guidance bubble out of alignment. That put us into an air spin and the port side wing cut through the waves. Salt spray pelted the window, reducing visibility to zero. I straightened out and the water fell away clearing my view again, and I saw a geological formation, a very big rock, looming directly in front of us. The twins squealed—not in delight this time. "Zap! Where did that come from?" I swerved deftly to avoid a smash-up.

I swung us around to get a better look and focused the navigation viewfinder. "Snap that," I told Dot, "And store the image in the future-collisions-to-avoid file."

Dot said, "We'll need three snapshots …"

"… to triangulate the precise location," and before I'd finished the sentence I'd pointed the Blast in a vertical course to capture a high-altitude view.

Lora and Lee both moaned. I thought I was making them airsick, so I leveled out. We were high enough, and I had Dot take a second snapshot.

Lora said, "Oh, genuine Gin."

"Fun's over." Lee said, and pointed to her glowing anklet.

"It's a Perry call," Lora said in a whiny, pleading voice, "Ginny-Gin,"

"Zip home, pronto." Lee sounded anxious, too.

I called up the course to Omega II. But before we zipped east, I took a brief moment to drop down and get a third snapshot of the beach rock we'd barely avoided. I stared at Dot's screen. Her notation indicated the rock was a crystalline outcropping of iron ore, and the rock looked even more massive than when I'd nearly clipped the Blast wing on it. I banked slightly to my starboard before scooting inland to Omega II and, here's the zapper, from this angle I could see a clear path through the middle of the iron rock. I shivered. The keyhole opening looked smooth, carved, obvious. Why hadn't any of us seen this before?

This rock was the missing arch from Great-gran Vera's book. I had stumbled upon the location of the hyperspace jump point to Earth.

⊕

Trapped Again

I slipped the Blast back into the Tree House cradle. The camp was dark and quiet, but Perry was waiting when we landed. He growled, "Taking a joy ride?"

Lora gasped, "Oh, very Perry."

"Don't be angry," Lee pleaded.

Zap. I was already a prisoner. How much more trouble could I get into? I stepped up and said, "I kidnapped your girls, but with their quick wits and wily ways they forced me to return to camp."

My explanation sounded ridiculous, even to me, but he accepted my admission of guilt. Perry grunted to the twins, "Cage her and get in," and he returned to the Skat ship.

Lora and Lee seemed relieved that I had taken the heat for our joy ride. They gave me all the sweets from their pockets, apologized for locking me up inside a cage, and skipped away.

I was trapped again but, whether deliberate or not, the twins neglected to throw an electromagnetic net over my cage. I could move! I waited until the other girls went inside their ship before I rattled the cage, testing my leverage. I tried rocking back and forth. If I could get a rhythm going and build momentum, I thought I could tip the whole thing over and escape.

Then I heard a familiar sound. *Meow*. It was Spooky, on a tree branch above me. Gordy was next to him, hanging onto a rope. He dropped down into my cage.

"Where have you been?" I asked.

"Successfully avoiding imprisonment," Gordy said. "Where have you been?"

"Building trust with our captors," I said.

"That's worked well for you," Gordy said.

"Why didn't you free all of us earlier with your demagnetizer?"

"The toy? I let one of the little kids have it," Gordy said. "I didn't know I'd need it to spring you from the Skats."

Good thing we didn't need a demagnetizer to get out of the cage this time. We pulled up on Gordy's rope and pulley system and into the Tree House.

In the shelter of our family space ship I showed him the image of the iron keyhole arch, the one Dot had snapped just south of Paraguin Cove.

Gordy said, "It looks exactly like the arch our Great-gran George drew."

"That's what I thought."

"You found the jump point!"

I still wasn't convinced that there was any such thing as a hyperspace jump. Not one feasible for transporting humans or other living creatures. My guarded response to his growing enthusiasm: "Maybe."

Gordy asked, "Don't you think it's strange that we didn't see the arch when we scouted the coastline before?"

"I think it was always there," I said. "But remember how much the level of the ocean water changes at the coast. At higher tides the arch shape was concealed."

Dot agreed, "Now the Tara moons are in an unusual astronomical alignment exerting a particularly strong gravitational pull. What we saw tonight at the beach is an extreme low tide that is still going out."

Gordy stared above the treetops at the pair of rising full moons. "Then tonight's the night to make the jump."

I whispered, "We have to tell Momo. She'll be so happy we found it."

Momo and Dad were still in the Skat's magnetic locks, standing back-to-back. Dad's hair was wild and he looked incredibly handsome. My dad the hero. My eyes started to burn again.

I asked Gordy, "Can you open the Skat lock?"

"The lock's no problem, but . . ." Gordy shook his head. "While you were out riding with your girlfriends, I tried. There's no way to get past the alarm curtains."

Zap. I walked around the cage.

It was especially tough to see Momo there, unable to move or talk. It was like the first time I'd seen her in the cryo tube. Even worse. Now she was vertical and she looked right at me. I knew she couldn't hear me, but I was desperate to say something, anything. I was just getting to know her again.

"We have to get them out," I said to Gordy.

"If we break the curtain to release Aunt Maureen and Uncle Leo, we'll set off the alarm," he said.

"I'm afraid to consider our other option."

"What other option?"

"Complete the mission." A soon as the thought came out of my mouth I tried to stop it. "Zap. No."

"That's what Aunt Maureen would tell us to do."

"You'd know. You're so tight with her." I realized I was being petty again, but doubt ruled everything coming out of my mouth. I was afraid ours was a lost cause, and our mission was over before we'd really begun. "We don't even know if the phytoplankton will work."

Gordy said, gently, "We may not get another chance."

I looked at Momo, and even in a magnetic lock she looked dynamic, like nothing could stop her. As much as it hurt me to leave Momo suspended in a cage, so against her nature, I knew Gordy was right. She would tell us to give it our best effort. We had to make the jump and carry the phytoplankton to Earth.

Even though I knew she couldn't hear me, I whispered to Momo, "Whatever happens, we'll come back and get you out."

⊕

250

⊕

The Keyhole Arch

I flew low to avoid detection, just in case one of the Skats was scanning for unidentified flying craft. When Gordy and I made it to Paraguin Cove the second moon rose high in the sky and the tide was even lower than it had been in my earlier ride with the twins. I turned south around the point and there it was, sitting dramatically on the sand: the iron archway.

Dot had done a statistical analysis on the variable differences between high and low tides, so it was clear how the arch formation regularly disappeared below the surface of the water. We might have seen rocks, but the distinctive keyhole arch was most often submerged. Now, at the lowest possible tide, the arch was fully exposed, and it was hard to believe none of us had seen it before.

"Ready to jump?" I asked.

Gordy took a deep breath, held Spooky close to his chest, and nodded.

I lined up the Blast with the keyhole, banked 90 degrees, and flew through the moonlit slot.

Nothing happened.

I hovered over the shiny sand. I knew it was silly to think that we would fly through an arch and instantly materialize on another planet in another solar system. I'd been the vocal skeptic. I certainly didn't believe in magic and, aside from an old drawing, there was no clear evidence behind a hyperspace jump point. But I was discouraged. Once Gordy and I had made the commitment to complete the mission, some part of me believed we could make it to Earth.

Dot said, "Let's review Great-gran Vera's manuscript. Perhaps there's something in the image that we didn't notice at first glance."

I landed the Blast near the keyhole arch so we could compare the drawing with the actual rock formation. Dot brought up George's map and, while I turned off the engines, Gordy unbuckled and bent over Dot's screen.

Gordy lifted Spooky out of the way and pointed, "Look here, on the inside face of the keyhole."

Dot enlarged the section. It was a picture etched in the ocean side of the stone, a human hand with an eye at the center of its palm. Poised on the tips of the long, delicate fingers was a flower blossom with the petals pointing upward.

Dot said, "The flower appears to be a fair representation of a lotus blossom. This is undoubtedly a symbol of Green Tara."

"Green Tara? As in the ancient goddess, not the current planet?" I said.

"Yes, wise student. You have become your own lotus blossom. Fear not," Dot said. "The goddess within will help you overcome the most difficult of situations."

"Dottie." I couldn't believe she was playing with character voices. We were trying to solve a real-life riddle. "It's not a good time to speak in Zen koans."

"You're referring to the wrong religious tradition," Dot said, reverting to her straight tutor voice. "In any case, my words are too specific to classify as a *koan*."

I wanted her to focus on our immediate situation. "I mean, your esoteric-ness isn't helping us!"

Gordy interrupted, "I think the goddess is pointing. If I'm right, the symbol is a direction arrow."

"What's she pointing to?" I asked. The rest of the arch just looked like a rock.

He shrugged, and Dottie blinked, speechless—a rare state for her. "Our virtual view isn't enough to crack this code." I wrapped Dot on my arm and popped the hatch, so we could get a closer look at the physical object.

Gordy tucked Spooky in his tunic along with a couple of oxygen hoods, "Just in case," he said, and hopped out first.

"You're an optimist." I followed him across the wet sand toward the arch.

We pried barnacles and seaweed away from the inside face of the keyhole looking for the symbols we saw in the drawing. A flock of paraguins landed nearby. Gordy clicked and whistled in response to their raucous chorus and the birds waddled around us.

"What are you saying?" I asked.

"It's just small talk. Look." He pointed to an exposed area of the iron. It was the symbol of Green Tara. "It's just like the drawing. At least that checks out."

Gordy and I cleared sand from all around the flower and fingers. He said, "Look. The Green Tara symbol is the handle of a dial."

"If the fingers are pointing like an arrow ..." I looked around the petals to see what else might be engraved on the arch. Less than a hand span away, I found another symbol carved in the iron.

"A cross inside a circle is the symbol for Earth, your ancestral home," Dot said. "It signifies the place where matter and spirit meet."

I looked closely at the symbol for Earth. The circle and cross design looked more organic than geometric, shaped with intricately woven ropes. I touched it, wondering if it would feel alive. The iron felt warm in the cool moonlight.

The paraguins closed in around us, and their song softened in a pleasing harmony.

Gordy reached up, too, and reverently held the hand of Green Tara. "If we rotate the symbol to the right, until the petals point to the circle and the cross...?" He looked at me for permission to test his theory. I knew what he was thinking, that the symbol was a control that operated a hyperspace jump point. It was a thin theory, but we had nothing to lose. I nodded for him to try it. He spun the hand without much apparent effort, and it clicked quietly into place.

Aside from the lotus blossom now leaning to the right, there was no visible difference around the archway. But as soon as the fingers and petals of Tara pointed to the circle and cross of Earth, all our movements were accompanied by a melodic hum. The paraguins swayed contentedly. The sound was lovely, and relaxing, but there was something else working at a deeper level. Something beyond the range of my hearing. A vibrational energy soaked into my pores.

Gordy and I stood with the ebbing tide sucking the sand from under our feet.

"Interesting," Dot said. "The entire arch seems to be resonating with the crystal core of the planet."

Gordy said, "You said the planetary core of Tara is iron and that's true of Earth, too. Maybe that's the connection that makes the hyperspace jump possible."

"Zap. I hear the start of a brilliant line of theoretical inquiry," I said, wondering how Gordy could be so cool and analytical about our discovery. Assuming this keyhole was a jump point—still, an untested phenomenon—we were talking about jumping to another planet!

A cold mechanical voice interrupted our impromptu science lesson. "Unauthorized personnel, attention!"

It sounded like the announcement system onboard our colonial cruiser—a timbre of voice we would never hear on our wildlife preserve.

Impossible!

At that moment a Triumvirate hovercraft appeared overhead. This was worse than the pirate invasion. Infinitely worse.

Zap.

The voice squawked again, "The Forbidden Zone is rated toxic. You are required to present your operating passes, and you must vacate immediately."

"Is this some kind of joke?" I really hated being interrupted. How dare some hopped up Trivert drones tell us what to do. This was my special family moment, and they were not going to interfere with our mission. Plus, ordering us to vacate a toxic zone was clearly irrational. I shouted up, "If this planet's ruined, we can't hurt it."

After a brief pause, the speaker said, "We are not protecting the Zone from your potential damage. The Zone is off limits to protect you."

"He's protecting us," Gordy said, facetiously, "I feel safer already."

The hovercraft lowered. A man in a gray jumpsuit, a Trivert sentry, stepped close enough to the edge that I could see him. "It is our duty to protect civilians from the dangerous environment." A second sentry turned on a searchlight that temporarily blinded me.

Dot chimed in, "According to Triumvirate Code 83-EZED, a sentry's primary duty is to protect property owned by the Triumvirate. Furthermore, I have scanned your one hundred and thirty-three other duties and I assure you that protecting civilians is not part of your duty list." Dot, true to her programming nature, was leveraging bureaucratic details to turn our transgression, trespassing on a supposedly toxic planet, into a non-issue. She was stalling for time, and it worked.

"This is highly irregular." A third sentry checked his tablet for the appropriate protocol.

The real issue, of course, was the absolute ban on any flights into the Zone, which we had ignored to rescue Momo in the first place. The irony was this small sentry craft was in the Zone, too. If it was so toxic and officially forbidden, what were they doing here?

"You do NOT have authorization to fly this Galaxy Blast here or anywhere." The first sentry leaned over the railing, close enough for me to recognize. It wasn't just any Triumvirate sentry. It was the MP who had interrogated me for flying the Blast without a license. "You are also in violation of Codes 3313 and 4337: Property Theft." With a sneer he said, "Add that to another unauthorized flight plan. You won't get off so easily this time."

"Sounds like he knows you," Gordy said.

The MP pointed a weapon at us, and something about his stance made me think it wasn't on a magnetic lock or stun setting. He was aiming to do permanent damage. "We're taking you into custody."

I stared up into his black eyes. He wasn't wearing his intimidating hat, but his eyes were scary beyond belief.

I'd just gotten out of a cage, and I didn't want to get into another one, certainly not under orders by this man. I looked at Gordy. So often he pulled out a tool or a toy to get us out of a tight spot, but I knew all he had with him was a small black kitten. I hoped he would come up with something.

He did. He whistled a peculiar trill, and hundreds of paraguins rose up from the sand, creating chaotic air currents all around us. The birds, our friends, heard his call for help and rushed the Triumvirate craft. The sentries scrambled as the flapping movement upset their hovercraft balance, tipping it at a radical 45-degree angle. The MP struggled to hold on and protect his face from claws and beaks.

This was our chance.

Before Gordy and I made the jump, we did something we hadn't done in a long time. We reached out to each other and held hands. And then, we stepped through the keyhole together.

⊕

Reseeding a Desolate Ocean

Gordy and I stepped from a moon-drenched beach onto a sunbaked bluff. In between footsteps the hyperspace jump didn't feel like a jump at all. It was more like every cell wall and energetic connection became fluid. When my body solidified again, I gazed over another sandy coast. Earth looked desolate compared to the planet we'd just left. Into the distance all I could see was desert. The only vegetation was scrub brush, the only life forms, hard-shelled insects. Scrappy life, tough enough to survive the harshest climate change.

Spooky meowed. He sounded pitiful. "That was a wild ride, wasn't it?" Gordy opened his tunic and let the kitten out. The oxygen hoods fell out, too. "But we made it to our destination and apparently don't need these to breathe." He stuffed the hoods back into an inner pocket.

Spooky chased insects and Gordy and I scanned the horizon of our ancestral planet. Behind us, on the other side of the keyhole arch the ocean moved rhythmically, much like what we knew on Tara. But the water here looked colorless and . . . dead.

We scrambled down the bluff and across a wide rocky beach. I wanted to take care of our mission and get back to Momo and Dad, so I wasted no time. I waded out waist-deep into the gray water. Gordy followed me.

"Dot." I peeled back her face flap. "Will our phytoplankton thrive here?" I dipped my fingers into the surf and dribbled sea water onto Dot's face.

"Nice and cool." Dot chimed. "Good news, Gin-Gin. The PH level is within range."

Gordy nodded.

"Then let's let the little green oxygen-makers get to work." I slipped the vial out of its sleeve, opened to let the contents thaw and, without ceremony, emptied it. We held our collective breath and watched the tiny stream of green water sink into the colorless ocean.

"It's probably unrealistic to think we could see the algae propagate instantly," I said.

Gordy nodded, clearly disappointed.

We sat at the edge of the vast ocean waiting to see what else might happen.

I buried my feet in the sand and watched the waves. Gordy explored tide pools with Spooky and collected ancient seashells that he stacked by my side.

As sunset neared Gordy returned with a handful of round, flat shells, something Dot identified as the skeletal remains of burrowing sea urchins, known to our ancestors as sand dollars. These were my favorites. But our mission wasn't going well. We still could not detect any change in the water.

I said, "Gordy. It's not working. The ocean is too big and too empty."

"We can't give up," he said, flopping in the sand. He made a sand angel. "The Earth's not completely dead."

"We don't have the power to heal it now." I made designs in the sand using Gordy's stack of seashells. Simple designs, an infinity symbol, a galaxy swirl. "Only one good thing. You're with me. I couldn't survive the disappointment alone."

"Gin, the sand's got energy. Don't you feel it? And the salt in the air. I can taste it."

"Yes, but . . ."

Gordy sat up. "If my mom's anything like yours . . . We have to find her, too." He squeezed his eyes shut.

I stroked Gordy's head and sang the first song that came to mind, the last song I'd heard him sing.

> "Old amber sparks and melts the juice.
> The deep sea breathes,
> Life blooms in salty water.
> Cool, clear water.
>
> It's time to sing for Mother Earth.
> The deep sea breathes,
> Each star's a pool of water.
> Cool, Clear water."

Gordy opened his eyes. "That's it." He jumped up and pulled the amber pendant off my neck.

"Gordy!"

"Gin, 'old amber'–it's a clue. It's what's missing."

"That's Dot's brain," I said, stretching for my amber pendant.

He held it up higher, just out of my reach. "Uncle Leo can build more bubble memory for Dot."

"More bubble memory won't be Dot." I pulled his arm down and took my pendant back. "It wouldn't have any of *her* memories."

Gordy said, "Gin, the amber is more than Dot's brain."

The amber in my hand grew warm and lit up. Dot's face shot out of it and shimmered in front of us. "Gordy is correct. Your amber pendant is more than my brain. There are enzymes embedded in the amber," she said. "By design it is the catalyst we need to incubate the phytoplankton."

"What?" I protested.

Dot's hologram dissolved from her face to Momo's letter, the one we'd found in Great-gran Vera's manuscript. At the very bottom she'd written, *P.S. I left the propagation catalyst with Dot.* My mind raced. When I'd first read the letter, I hadn't understood the meaning of this last sentence. Now, the meaning terrified me. By definition, a catalyst is destroyed by the process it activates. "I'm not throwing you away."

"Surely you understand." The hologram shimmered again and Dot's face reappeared. "My reason for being *is* to heal the water. This is why I was created."

"No. I will not throw you into the water and watch you dissolve. Momo and Dad both have amber pendants." Now that I understood the pendant design, I was certain they had implanted the same catalyst in their PIRSD operating systems, too. "We'll use one of theirs."

"Virginia, we may not get another opportunity," Dot said.

"You and I . . ."

"We've been very close. But you don't need me. You have Momo again."

"Momo?" Momo wasn't a substitute for Dot. I told Dot everything. I couldn't talk to my mother. I wanted to, but so far that hadn't worked out very well. "Having Momo's not the same."

"Having Momo is better," she said.

"No. Dottie." This was impossible. I didn't want to choose who was 'better'.

"It is time, Gin. Let go of your anger toward your mother. Let it go. Let me go." Dot's face evaporated.

I wasn't ready to give her up. I stumbled away from the surf, wading through a string of tide pools. Wherever I stepped the water looked . . . empty. I paused. At the bottom of another crystal clear pool, I saw seashells and sand dollars. Not life itself, but remnants of life.

Gordy appeared beside me.

"Wait," I whispered, holding the amber pendant in a double fist close to my body. "Gordy, it's not just a personal information retrieval and storage device with transportable and omniscient data. It's Dottie. It's more than her brain. It's her heart."

He said, "I know."

I breathed deeply and opened my cupped hands, holding them over the clear tide pool. Gordy opened his vial of phytoplankton and poured the living, green water over the amber. Reverently, I laid the amber among the seashells and sand dollars.

I brushed her, still warm on my arm, and kissed her soft polka dots. Dot. Dot. Dot. But I didn't dare open her flap. I couldn't say good-bye. The amber floated a few centimeters up, held down only by the weight of the chain. Gordy and I sat down on our knees, by the edge of the pool, and watched.

I held my breath. Perhaps nothing would happen, and all of Dot would still be mine.

In the salty water, the amber began to sparkle. Energy vectors shot out and burst into arcs of colored light. More and more little bursts filled the water with a dazzling light show. Then, as quickly as it had begun, all the color faded. The dance was over, and nothing was left. The amber had melted away, too. There was nothing. Nothing.

I'd sacrificed Dot for nothing!

I reached in, as if I could retrieve her from the empty water. But I couldn't.

I wrapped Dot's cold, limp flex form around my neck, and collapsed on the sand.

⊕

Bugs in the Tide Pool

I woke the next morning, crusty from a night on the sand. The first thing I saw was Spooky batting at the edge of the tide pool. All across the surface, bugs skittered around green foamy stuff. Gordy said, "Gin. Insects are diving in the water for their breakfast!" I blinked my eyes and sat up. Simple, sweet algae. The phytoplankton had propagated overnight!

"The phytoplankton. It's alive, Dottie. It worked." And then I remembered that Dot wouldn't respond. We had the most important accomplishment in my whole life to celebrate, and she couldn't hear me. Not anymore.

"Gin!" Gordy pulled me to the next pool. "The tide's coming in, and it's spreading."

It was true. The algae spread with each rolling wave.

Gordy cheered. Just for good measure, he sprinkled the last drops of green water from his vial and he ran, splashing along the shoreline.

Water sparkled in the sunlight and a cloud formed in the sky. The next wave exploded in brilliant color.

Aqua, magenta, deep violet, and gold. The transformation was stunning.

I knew that the colors of the microscopic phytoplankton would be invisible to the human eye, so I have no explanation for being able to *see* the energy of new life. Maybe the hyperspace jump had reset my senses.

Then, a double rainbow appeared over the water. It's a scientific fact that a rainbow is a prism effect of visible light. I'd seen the phenomenon on Tara, and Dot had explained light refraction through water suspended in the atmosphere. But a double rainbow at exactly this time and place? A double rainbow was quite rare. My heart sped up. I felt confident that our mission was complete.

⊕

⊕

Return to Green Tara

Gordy tucked Spooky back inside his tunic for our return trip. The day before on Tara, Gordy had turned the lotus petals to point toward the Earth symbol, and that had activated the connection between planets. Inside Earth's keyhole arch the same symbols were visible in reversed positions. The cross inside the circle, Earth, was on the dial. Gordy turned it, aiming the most decorative point of the cross toward the Green Tara lotus flower.

We had no guarantee that the jump point would work again and simultaneously keep both time and space stable. But the arch resonated, just as it had on the Tara beach, and that was a comforting feeling. I took his hand in mine and we stepped through together.

I felt the same pleasant sensation I'd experienced during our first jump, like all boundaries dissolved and every part of my body, including my mind, became tiny pieces in a fantastic mosaic of everything, everywhere. This feeling lasted for no time at all, yet it felt like forever. It was impossible to tell how long the jump took, because time had become irrelevant.

The shred of me that was conscious that I was part of all consciousness wondered if this was the state of *Being One* that religious mystics referred to. I would have asked Dot, but she was gone. I might have dwelled on loss, but in my state of being part of everything and nothing it was natural to accept all that was without attaching feelings of sadness. Interesting. And then my body and mind coalesced into its individual form again.

I could feel my hand where it touched Gordy's as we entered the keyhole arch on Green Tara. This time though, instead of a seamless stride through to the other side, it felt like hitting a wall.

After the brutal impact I saw beautiful, colorful creatures, some fat, some thin, some speckled, and some smooth moving all around me, and I felt myself being pulled gently, rhythmically. The floating sensation was almost as pleasant as the jump. I felt my empty fingertips. I'd lost Gordy. There he was, above me, outlined by sunlight.

I was underwater. Gordy reached down, tugged at my shoulder and pulled me up toward him.

I never lost consciousness, but I wasn't fully functioning, yet. The first thing I was clear about was sitting with Gordy. My clothes were still wet and his were, too. He said, "Good thing I learned to swim."

I was still disoriented. But I knew by the pungent smells that we were back on Tara. I looked around. The archway wasn't visible and I wondered where we had landed.

As if he knew the question on my mind, Gordy said, "The tide is up, Gin. When we returned we walked right into a wave. Catch your breath, and I'll get the Blast ready."

He and Spooky trotted across the sand. We were on a sliver of beach just south of Paraguin Cove and from the position of the sun, low over the water, I knew it was late in the day. But I had no idea how to factor in the time and space slip to know exactly *when* we had returned to Tara. I opened Dot to ask her to calculate . . . I knew she wouldn't be able to talk back, but reaching for her was a very old habit for me.

I took a deep breath of salt air and wiggled my toes and fingers in the warm sand. Every next move, thought, decision, I'd have to make without Dot. I stroked her silent flex form, still wrapped around my arm.

Gordy whistled from the back hatch of the Blast. He waved and ducked inside, ready for the next phase of our mission. I knew I couldn't wallow in my grief forever. That's what Dot would have said. I had to join him. After all, I was the pilot.

Then I felt the hair on the back of my neck rise and I heard a distinct, metallic clicking sound. Even without looking, I knew I was being watched. I gathered all my strength and in one swift move, I twisted around with a fistful of sand and slung it into the hovering SensEye.

It blinked and stalled, then reacted with a fit of shaking and shuttering hyperactivity, throwing itself out of balance. I'd never seen a SensEye change altitude so radically. It shot up high into the open sky. It seemed to stick to the bottom of a fluffy cloud. Then the eye plummeted twice as fast downward, disappearing into the water. Before the splash had completely settled, it bobbed up to the surface, and it rode the tide out to deeper water.

"Looks like its directional hardware has been soaked," I said to Dot. Then I remembered once again that Dot couldn't hear. I also remembered the Triumvirate sentries that chased after us just before our jump to Earth. Now that I'd been spied, they'd be back to our beach for sure. No time for sad thoughts. I scrambled to the Blast and closed the hatch behind me.

Gordy stood up from the storage bin. "Gin, I thought you might want some fresh water." He handed me a cup and straw.

"Thanks, Gordy. Let's jet." I strapped myself into the pilot's seat. "We've still got visitors."

I opened the Blast's ion engines and lifted off the sand just in time. The Triumvirate hover craft spun over the rocky cliff and into view. I was eyeball to eyeball with the other pilot, the MP who had held me in lockdown barely a fortnight ago! Zap.

"They're still here." Gordy said, "I was wondering if we'd have any time slippage during our jumps."

"Apparently not," I said. "Our Triverts look like they've been scouring the coastline for us while we were on Earth." I wished we had the luxury to ponder space-time phenomenon, but the MP looked peeved in the time frame of NOW. He was unshaven, and possibly had had no sleep over night.

He spoke directly into my headset, "Little Miss Bosque, flying without a license again? I do believe I've caught you violating a number of regulations. You always think you're going to get away with something. Now why don't you set your little Galaxy down before you get yourself hurt?"

I had a snarky remark about his recent tumble with the paraguins in mind—after all, I was wet and cranky too—but I restrained myself and said simply, "No thanks," dipped under the Triumvirate hovercraft and arced over the mountaintop, flying inland.

The MP spun lazily around and, once re-oriented, followed the Blast at a surprisingly fast pace. I raced just above the treetops, stirring up branches and leaves, hoping to create enough turbulence to destabilize the hovercraft.

Gordy said, "Looks like they're flying one of Leo's designs."

"Zap," I said. "I need Dot to get us out of this one."

"Things just got Skat-o-logical," Gordy said, pointing up ahead.

A V-shaped skimmer lifted up out of a deep gorge. Perry and the twins were visible in the cockpit. The skinny pirate sat high in a back gunnery. More people to outrun! What were the odds? It's like everybody in the galaxy had shown up on this one remote coastline, hidden in the Forbidden Zone, just to chase us.

I didn't have time to think up a perfect plan, so I did what I knew—the infinity chase, the pattern I'd perfected on my first test flight—the joy ride that had started this whole adventure. I spun my Blast around and raced back, crossing my own flight path, and then spun around again. Both the Triumvirate hovercraft and the Skat skimmer followed me into my infinity chase pattern. Tighter and tighter I wove the chase. And at the same time I spiraled down in elevation, inside the gorge. The deeper we went, the narrower the space between the gorge walls. I turned more sharply than I'd ever tried in deep space, racing faster and faster.

The landscape was a blur, but I was calm.

Until the north side cliff exploded. The Triumvirate hovercraft hadn't made the last turn and it had crashed, lighting up the shady gorge with flaming debris. "Oh, no," I gasped. I hadn't intended for anyone to get hurt. Once the scattered fragments dropped away, I pulled my Blast next to the smoldering crash site and stared. There wasn't much left.

Gordy pointed up, "Look."

Up above the cliff face we could see three parachutes with a Triumvirate sentry dangling from each one. I felt relieved. The Skat skimmer landed on an outcropping just below them, and the skinny pirate aimed a magnetronic beam at one of the sentries and pulled him in, I knew the sentries were safe—but not *in control*. Perfect.

"If the Skat's threw a security net over you, imagine what they'll do to the sentries," Gordy laughed.

The twins were out of the skimmer ready to seize the sentry as he dropped to the ground. Even though I couldn't hear them, as the girls untangled the man from his parachute lines I could imagine them giggling about their

Trivert catch. The skinny pirate caught the second sentry and pulled him toward the outcropping, too.

I saw the last man, the MP, sweep past. Only, he was no longer drifting from his parachute lines. He was moving horizontally, courtesy of an ion-powered backpack, and he pointed directly at me. "You're still under arrest, little Miss Bosque," he hissed into a mouthpiece and into my headset. Then he jetted north.

"I'm not sure if we should chase him or run," I said as casually as I could. The adrenaline rush made me giddy. I was tempted to laugh at the absurd MP. I could have just as easily cried in relief that we'd managed to evade Triumvirate rule.

"Let the Skats take care of him," Gordy pointed below. The skinny pirate already had his magnetron gun aimed at the fleeing MP.

I nodded and said, "Next stop: Omega II." We still had a mother and a father to rescue, so I turned the Blast eastward and flew just above the treetops, joining in formation with a flock of purple cranes.

⊕

⊕

Rescuing Momo – Again

As we approached Omega II, I developed a plan: drop silently through the trees and back into the Tree House cradle without triggering any of the pirates' ground sensors. Also, this landing spot would put us above my parents' cage. After that, my plan was a little sketchy, but the desired outcome was clear: rescue Momo and Dad, and fly away undetected.

I executed a perfect landing into the Tree House. Gordy exited the Blast first, and I slid out the back hatch after him. Just as I touched the ground, I realized Dot was still on the console where I'd spread her out to dry. Even though she was no longer functional, I missed her soft touch, and I crawled back up inside to get her. "Be right out, Gordy." But before I could retrieve Dot, I heard Lora and Lee giggle.

"Bosque kiddles." I stooped to clear the hatch opening and saw the twins below. "Gotcha." They each grabbed one of Gordy's hands. They giggled again, and simultaneously raised their outer palms, striking a pose.

My heart dropped. I couldn't tell what the twins had in mind. Were they doing a victory celebration pose?

As in, *gotcha again. You're my slave.* Dad had warned me they were unpredictable. In my momentary panic, I blurted, "We're not your enemy. The TriVerts are the real threat."

"We know, girlie," Lora said, sweetly.

Lee finished. "But you and boy wonder—come." They beckoned to me, a gentle gesture without weapons or a threat. Gordy was sandwiched between them, but he looked relaxed.

The knot in my gut loosened. I hoped for all our sake's, the Skats would be our allies.

The twins linked arms with Gordy and me and led us past the cage where Dad and Momo were still immobilized by the magnetic lock. Dad's head faced the opposite direction, but Momo could see me wave to her, and I was pretty sure I saw relief in her eyes.

At the center of the clearing, three Skats huddled near a cluster of antennas and transmitters.

"Ginnie-Gin's here," Lora announced.

"Gord-o-riffic, too," Lee sang out.

Perry stood up and motioned us to come closer. "Here." He held up a small screen so we could all see the image: a blip moving northward.

"The Tri-Vert M.P?" I asked rhetorically. Who else could it be? "I thought you'd captured them all."

He snorted, "Tagged him, but our magnetron grab failed. Now he's out of skim range." He pointed back to the screen and we watched the blip move into a vast open area beyond the forest. The blip slowed and then stopped. Perry asked Gordy, "Kiddle, can you lift a Tri-Vert sig?"

Gordy nodded. "Put his eye on, so we see what he's about."

Gordy nodded again, took the handheld screen, and played with the controls under his fingers. It didn't take much for him to unlock the MP's SensEye and maneuver it so we had a decent view. What we saw surprised us all: A three-sided craft rising straight up from the northern tundra.

Gordy said, "He's got a Triumvirate Patrol Glider."

"Also called a Tri-Pod Glider, for short," I said.

"Interstellar?" Perry asked.

Gordy nodded. "Perfectly equipped."

"It's my dad's design, and it's good," I said.

The Tri-Pod Glider rose rapidly through the clouds. The MP had obviously stopped searching for us. Instead, he was approaching escape velocity.

"He's leaving Tara." Gordy said

"We can't let him return to the cruiser or any other Triumvirate post. He knows all about Green Tara. The wildlife sanctuary will fall to Corporate ownership rules." I begged Perry. "We can't let that happen."

"Our ship's all nuts and bolts. Maintenance time." Perry waved his hand at the hastily improvised communication network. "Can't stop him."

"My dad can stop him," I said.

"She's right. Uncle Leo will know how to disable the craft," Gordy said.

"You've got to let him loose. My dad's not your enemy. The Tri-Verts are." I pointed at the rising blip. "The MP will bring back more and they'll lock us all up, and everything here on the planet, too. They don't know how to live with the wilderness, only how to own and control creatures."

Perry appeared to be listening.

"The Verts use their rules to control everything and everyone in the galaxy, including the Skats. Free my parents, and they will help you." I tried again to convince him to let my parents go. "Remember, my dad can set you up with a free powered water generator."

My persuasive argument worked. Sort of.

Perry agreed to release Dad, but not Momo. Not yet. Her freedom was contingent on his success. Ultimately, the fate of the whole family depended on Dad's ability to thwart the Triumvirate MP.

The skinny pirate unlocked Dad from his cage, and Gordy and I explained the urgent situation. Dad knew exactly what to do. We all followed him, climbing up to the Tree House and crowding into the cockpit of his String Machine.

Perry and Gordy and I watched over Dad's shoulder. I was desperately hoping the MP was still in range and that Dad could disable his ship.

The Tri-Pod Glider was climbing out of Green Tara's outer atmosphere, when Dad leaned back in his chair and sighed with satisfaction. "I've infected his navigation system."

Perry said, "Lost without a rudder."

"Not entirely," Dad said. "The Tri-Pod Glider is still operational. It'll take him through the uncharted Zone near enough to the cruiser to pick up a beacon signal and follow it to the home ship. But as soon as he locks onto the beacon, the virus will trigger a corruption sequence. It'll wipe out his entire flight history, and he won't have any way to trace back to the Tara system."

Everyone else nodded, satisfied that the MP was no longer a problem. They squeezed out of the cockpit and gathered in the main chamber of the Tree House.

I followed. "But Dad, he found Tara once," I said.

"He wasn't looking for Tara, though." Dad explained, "He got here by following a tracer signal that he'd planted on my personal ship. I found and disabled the tracer chip after landing here. That MP was able to follow me, but without a flight record he won't be able to find Green Tara again."

"But he'll tell the Director of the Board and then we'll have the entire Triumvirate looking for us," I said.

"I don't think so," said Dad. "The MP was flying my prototype, a ship I personally own, on an unauthorized flight plan."

"Rogue thief," Perry said, smugly, labeling the MP as the worst kind of outlaw. "Worse than a rebel Skat."

Dad nodded. "If the MP doesn't return to the cruiser with evidence, hostages or hard information about Tara's location, he won't go to the Director. As it is, he'll have a rough time explaining why he's flying a stolen craft. Though, he might claim he commandeered my Tri-Pod Glider to try to catch two runaway sentries."

Everyone else seemed satisfied with Dad's reassurance. But I'd seen the vengeful look in the MP's eyes, and I completely understood his motivation to catch

Dad *and me* defying Triumvirate regulations. Now that we'd thwarted him again, I was fairly certain I was on the top of his zap list. "So, he's no real threat?" I asked, still not entirely convinced.

"No. Not now he isn't." Dad grinned, "How about a hug?" He took both me and Gordy into his burly arms.

"What about you, Dad?' I said, "Won't they send an official search team for you?"

"I'm sure they did," he said, and that conjured up visions of endless Triumvirate invasions in my mind. Dad chuckled, "Don't worry, sweetheart. I left a distress signal on a rocky asteroid."

"A false trail!" said Gordy.

Dad nodded and said, "I left scrap jet parts scattered around a burned out crater, just enough to look like my String Machine exploded."

"You faked your death?" I said. Perry roared with laughter.

Dad nodded and kissed the top of my head. After a good long squeeze he set us down and said, "I know it was your home, but there's no going back for any of us, ever."

I think he was apologizing, but I was relieved. I didn't miss the colonial cruise ship, *at all*. Green Tara, with all its wacky smells, felt more like home than anywhere, except maybe a tide pool on Earth.

"No problem, Uncle Leo, we are home." Gordy hopped in a hammock. "Our Tree House is the best home in the galaxy!"

Gordy was right, and I was done worrying about Triumvirate retribution. Only one thing was missing to make our home complete. "We have to get Momo." I looked at Perry, "You'll let her free now. You promised."

"Deal's a deal," Perry said.

⊕

Me, the Brilliant Negotiator

As soon as the tall skinny Skat unlocked the security net, I grabbed Momo's hand and pulled her out of the cage.

She hugged me and the first thing she said was, "Gin, you're brilliant. You negotiated our release."

Dad said, "Right, Gin. Your trade offer—brilliant." He sounded proud. They both did.

It was nice to be recognized, but my negotiation skills wouldn't have counted for anything if Dad hadn't been able to disable the Tri-Pod Glider navigation. "It was you, Dad, and what you did, because earlier, when I tried to trade..."

Before I finished my sentence, Dad kissed Momo on the lips.

I squirmed, "Earlier, I offered the Skats a water generator." But I don't think Dad or Momo was listening.

"Trade offer—accepted." Perry and his man ambled toward the Skat ship.

"Good thing the generator is portable, it'll be perfect for the beach party," Gordy said.

"You've had time to plan a beach party?" I asked, bewildered by the random topic.

"The colonists did," Gordy nodded. He pulled a message disk from his pocket. "To celebrate their new home, the Skat's last supper on Tara, and our jump."

Momo tuned back to us, "Your jump?"

"While you were locked in the security net," I said.

"Virginia found George's Keyhole Arch just south of Paraguin Cove. That's why we're still a little damp," Gordy said. "The tide came up and..."

"You took the phytoplankton?" Momo asked. "To Earth?" Even though Gordy had clearly said that I had found the jump point, Momo's attention was locked on Gordy.

Gordy looked to me, and I remembered the sparkling tide pool, the rainbow, and Spooky playing with the propagating algae. The whole amazing journey. But, I also remembered sacrificing Dot, and my throat tightened. I lost my voice.

"Those tiny green oxygen generators are alive and thriving on their planet of origin," Gordy spoke for both of us. "Aunt Maureen, the Earth Restoration project has powered up!"

"It worked." Momo whispered back to Gordy, "You made it work, and you're already back with us." She sounded surprised. And her intimate conversation with him made it seem like he was the one who led the mission. True, he's the one who found the words, but I couldn't stand that her focus had shifted so dramatically from me, her daughter, to him.

Meanwhile, he joked, "You didn't believe we could do it?"

Momo said, "Of course, I believed. But how did you … ?"

Before her question was fully formed, he cartwheeled across the clearing toward the outdoor kitchen and yelled, "That's what we're celebrating!"

I completely acknowledge that Gordy was a full participant in our mission. I couldn't have done it without him. Not any of it. I wouldn't have been brave enough to jump alone. I would have given up too soon. I would have drowned on re-entry. But—I WAS THERE, TOO. "You want to know how we did it?" I cried, "I sacrificed Dot."

My mother looked at me, stunned. "Dot?" Like she didn't know or care what I was talking about.

I didn't have the patience to explain everything that Gordy and I had done, or how we'd figured out the clue in the folk song, and that Dot—my best friend forever and ever—had said having Momo back was better. For the first time in my entire life Dot had been wrong. Dot had always understood everything. Momo didn't get it, at all. Our mother-daughter love fest fell apart before it even began.

I ran deep into the woods looking for a place where I felt safe.

Every human on the planet gathered on the beach near the Omega I site. The high tide had turned and was on its way out, and the sun was approaching its watery setting. The light was stunning, the salty air tasted delicious, and everyone was jolly—everyone except for me.

I overheard some colonists whisper about my glum mood. They seemed to think it was related to the hyperspace jump. But they were wrong, and their gossiping just made my skin prickle. Earth was easy compared to being with my family. Even though several days had passed since the latest fallout with my mother, that primary emotional disconnect was the source of my foul mood. Dad said I was being anti-social. I just didn't want to be around anyone. The more others laughed and played, the more I wanted to hide.

The beach party scene was particularly difficult. I had to escape. So I climbed the small bluff to get away from the crowd, and then crawled up through the back hatch into my Galaxy Blast. All I wanted was to be alone.

Zap! Inside my mother was sitting in the co-pilot's seat with Dot stretched across her lap. This unexpected meeting was awkward—understatement. I couldn't think of anything to say.

Momo broke the silence, "Hello, Gin. Here." She stood and wrapped Dot around my shoulders.

I stroked Dot's plush side. I missed her so much. I had to blame somebody, so I shouted at Momo, "Why didn't you tell me what it would take?"

"I thought it would be my amber pendant. I thought it would be me sacrificing Zoe. I'm so sorry." Momo stood for a long time with her apology hanging in the air.

I stood silent.

"The good news is before you left Tara, Dot downloaded everything she had into your Blast's memory banks," Momo said. "She assumed you'd want her back-up files."

"Everything?" I whispered.

"All the data, all your logs." Momo nodded. "I've already rebuilt her framework. It'll be up to her to rebuild her neural processing pathways. That, as you probably know, could take considerable time."

"She won't ever be the same," I said.

"No, she won't. Not exactly. Her personality will evolve differently. But she'll still be your Dot." Momo handed me an emerald green pendant, the new processor. "When you're ready, call her up." She slipped quietly out the back hatch.

I buried my face in Dot's softness and whispered, "Dot? Are you really there?"

"Of course, I'm here," Dot said. "Now put my new pendant on and go apologize to your mother."

"For what?"

"You've been disrespectful," she said, her tutor voice completely reset.

"How do you know?" Dot rolled her eyes. Apparently her sensors were working. But just because she was back up to speed, I wasn't ready to submit to every command. "How can anything I do or say be *disrespectful*? She lost full motherhood status a decade ago."

"That's not how I remember it," Dot said.

"What do you remember?"

Dot blinked dreamy water-color eyes, and out of them a memory scene rose up in front of me. I was a little girl. And Momo held out a present to her girl, me, little Virginia.

I remembered this. It was my birthday party, and the little girl in the picture was me on the day I turned five. Dot had shown me the recording before, but a different part, when I'd gotten her, my PIRSD, my Dot. In this part of the recording Momo pulled open the drawstring of a velvet bag. My eyes grew round, and I clapped as she pulled out a shiny toy space ship. Momo laughed and held me up high, spinning me around in the air, while I flew the ship. "Zip Ziparee!" Faster and faster we spun around until we tumbled to the floor.

We giggled and snuggled and Momo whispered, "You're my bright star, destined to chart the galaxy."

"Thank you, Momo." Little Virginia planted a firm kiss on Momo's lips, and the memory froze.

"Your mother has always believed in you," Dot said.

Dot was right. Momo had known I had a passion for flying even before I understood my own nature.

"I think it's time for you to give her credit for what she's done right."

"Oh, Dottie." I wiped my eyes—When had they gotten hot again?—and wrapped Dot around my arm. "Let's join the party and find Momo."

⊕

The Beach Party

By the time the setting sun slipped into the ocean, the first annual Green Tara Beach Party was well under way. The colonists supplied food, and several pirates played musical instruments. Even the Triumvirate sentries were there, the pair who'd been captured. They were tasked with building a giant bonfire. The whole festive gathering felt unexpected and perfect, for the unexpected and perfect planet, Green Tara.

I watched Lora juggle gold coins for entertainment. "No one can resist . . ."

". . . an authentic pirate doubloon," Lee giggled as Gordy caught a coin in mid-air and dashed away.

On the other side of the bonfire Gordy offered the gold coin to Perry. As the flames leapt higher, I wondered if they were talking about Gordy's mother, and if the leader of the Skats had any information about her that he would share with Gordy. The success of our mission was being celebrated, but Aunt Celia was still missing. Driftwood in the fire popped and moaned.

"Ginny-Gin!" Lora chirped.

"Ace pilot," Lee giggled again, and took my arm for a little prance.

"Master of the electrical storm disguise." Lora said, pocketing her coins.

"We let you slip away," Lee whispered.

"So we could follow," Lora said.

"And see what you wanted to see," Lee said, leading me to a table where party supplies were stacked.

"You know what's valuable," Lora said.

"The water you brought us—priceless," Lee said, letting me go.

Lora opened a small box and held out a headband adorned with a brilliant orange plume. I ran my finger along the edge, still amazed by the soft tickle so unique to a bird's feather. Lee slipped it onto my head, and the twins bowed. I hadn't expected any kind of present. I knew they were thanking me, and I thought I should be thanking them—for their friendship and loyalty. But words didn't seem important. The girls smiled, locked arms at their elbows and danced around the blazing bonfire.

In a quiet moment between songs I heard one of the sentries speak, "I've always wanted the life of a settler." He was eyeing the bountiful fruit and a pretty girl on the colonists' side of the camp ring.

"Good choice," I said, uncertain why I cared what happened to the man who had tried to capture me. But I did care, and it seemed like the colonists could use all the help they could get. The sentry discarded his uniform jacket and joined the settlers. They pounded him heartily on the back and gave him a place in the circle.

That brought attention to the other sentry, who backed away from the colonists.

"You don't look like much of a settler, son," the eldest colonist said.

An anonymous voice joked, "Drop him off on another continent."

Another piped in, " ... and let him go solo."

The eldest stood, and she said, "We are no longer bound by Triumvirate law. This man is free now."

"I . . . I . . . ," the sentry stuttered, "I've always dreamed . . ." He looked at his feet.

Another colonist prompted, "You're a free man. What do you want?"

"To be free to roam the stars like the Skats," the former Triumvirate sentry confessed.

The Skats roared their approval. They lifted their new comrade on their shoulders and paraded him around the camp circle.

Everyone mingled and laughed. It was a grand party. Dad was teaching a couple of kids dance steps he knew. But I didn't see Momo, and what I wanted most was to find her.

Far from the bonfire, crouched down where the waves lapped at my toes, I nuzzled Dot's plush side and whispered, "Dot, are you there?" Dot purred, and I sat straight up. "Dottie, you remember how to purr."

"I can crow, too. My cache memory is quite robust," Dot said.

"Show me something." I lifted Dot's flap.

"I would like to. I have something you haven't opened, yet."

There was a message icon on Dot's screen. I touched it, and Ray appeared. "Virginia, first of all, I'm going through channels that can't be traced. And before, I didn't . . . Please accept my calls again. I'm no traitor. I'm . . . I'm sorry. Please let me know you're safe."

Dot asked, "Your reply?"

"No reply," I said. "Not now. Not now." I saw Momo walking along the water line.

I skittered in the foam and caught up to her. "Momo, I've been thinking about our mission. When do we start incubating fish eggs for Earth?"

Momo laughed. "The colonists will handle repopulating fish and krill. We have another task ahead of us."

"What?" I asked, thinking she might have another dozen planets to rescue.

"It's time to build a sand castle," Momo said.

"What's that?" I asked.

"Come on. I'll show you." Momo knelt in the wet sand and dug a moat. She showed me how to build a fortified wall, and once the basic structure was up we added details, a drawbridge made from a flat stone and shell designs pressed into the sand. Momo added a flag to the top of the tower, a striped paraguin feather I found on the beach.

"Sweet." The sand castle was complete, and we laid back to gaze at the night sky. As if celebrating, too, the sky exploded with shooting stars and big, blazing bolides. When the show subsided I confessed, "I still call you Momo, but it's so strange. I'm sorry I get so angry with you. It's odd ..."

"What's odd?" asked Momo, very gently.

I hesitated, and finally confessed what I'd been thinking, "You're my Momo, but you don't feel like a mother."

"No," Momo said. She sounded sad. "I've missed so much time with you."

I didn't want to feel sad about what we'd missed. Not anymore. I wanted to simply be with her now. "So, what *does* it feel like? I mean for you, being with me. Is it like being with your sister, Celia?"

"No. Yes. It's more than the fact that you look like my sister. You're not Celia. But, you and I—it's odd—we're so close in age now, it feels more like we're sisters."

"Like sisters." I smiled.

"Not exactly. We're definitely family," she said.

"Definitely." My face relaxed, and I breathed in the salty spray.

"I love that you still call me Momo," she whispered.

"Me, too, Momo," I whispered back.

A bit of ocean swirled into the moat. The tide had turned and was coming in again.

We stood together and ran into the foam, dancing in the living, breathing water.

⊕

⊕

New Dot Log

Dot log: Zero years, zero months, 21 days

Dear Dot,

Dad continues to create in his typical dad-like style. Inspired by the exoskeletons of the native insects, he and the Skat glassblower fashioned a bubble of silicate compound over the metal framework of the Tree House. It's a simple invention—as he says, the best inventions are so often very simple—and our tandem space ship with a clear bubble shell is, without a doubt, the most unique ship in the galaxy.

First thing this morning the Skats carried their water generator and all the fresh fruit they could handle, courtesy of the colonists, to their ship. Perry and the twins were the last on board. The three saluted us. It was a goofy gesture that, coming from them, was strangely touching. Then they stepped through their open cargo bay and took flight. The edge of the upper atmosphere unzipped, and the Skats disappeared in a blue flash. I suspect Dad learned more than bubble blowing tricks from them.

Then it was our turn to prep for take-off. Practicing sisterhood, Momo and I coordinated the tricky lift off, straight up and out of the cradle of tree limbs. Even though we'd never flown together before, we maneuvered the awkward situation from two separate cockpits. Liftoff was flawless. Momo said it's because we know each other on a cellular level. We made one last pass over the new settlement and the colonists waved good-bye.

I pressed my face against the window for one last look at the shimmering clouds and ocean water of Green Tara. Gordy, in the co-pilot's seat, couldn't bear to watch the planet surface get further and further away. His voice may have dropped, and he's the bravest person I know, but he's also the most tender-hearted. He buried his face in Spooky's fur.

Dad made some final engineering adjustments and, sooner than I expected, Momo announced over the headsets, "Get ready for interstellar space." The Tree

House lifted out of orbit, and I gazed at lovely Tara, rapidly receding in space.

This is it, Dot. Our family has launched the next phase of our mission: We're on our way to rescue Gordy's mom.

the end

⊕

Acknowledgements

I begin by thanking my family, for they are my first audience, often hearing ideas lurking in the corners of my mind, not yet ready to be scribbled on a napkin. They've endured endless drafts, character name changes, and agonizing decisions over chapters to be sacrificed. My Dad was the first person who named my gift of writing, long before I took myself seriously. My sisters and brothers have all cheered me on. Sharon, Scott, Heather, and Minor, I'm so grateful you are in my life. My nieces, Lindsey, Candace, and Mallory, have listened to story pitches and read early drafts, always giving me the green light.

My children have grown up with this story and, without a doubt my characters share elements of their fierce attitude and infinite intelligence. Whatever you find authentic about Virginia and Gordy and their relationship, you will recognize when you meet Haley and Wynn. My husband, Bill, has always supported my creative life. Without him, none of this would be possible. Thank you, for your faith and love.

Over the years, many have encouraged my creative activity with the generosity of their time to read my stories and with votes of confidence that my vision is worthy of an audience. Thank you, Nancy Hausauer, Gail Hale, Michael Ford, Christina Anderson, Danielle McClelland, Tonia Mathews, Elizabeth Simiri, Jim Fisher, Janet Bell, Jennifer VanSijll, Jim & Luci McKean, Joe & Meridee LaMantia, Marybeth Kelsey, Min Gates, Nancy Schwartz, Rich Lewis, Ros Johanna, Beth Mink, Susan Sullivan, Terrie Page, Thom & Dori Gillespie, Lauri Boyd, Nancy Macklin, Lee Sheldon, Sasha Barab, Tonia Mathews, Christy Cavanaugh, Dan Nelson, Scott Russell Sanders, Anna Lynch, Beth Pierkarsky and her class of 5th graders at University Elementary.

Dr. Jose Bonner spent many hours discussing with me how terraforming could actually work, keeping in mind the principles of evolutionary biology, so that I could create a world that is guided by scientific principles even though I make no claims of delivering hard science fact. Rea Kersey, illustrator extraordinaire, has visualized the story world and made it more vibrant than words can express.

I'd also like to give a collective shout out to my former Indiana University students, who taught me all the tough questions, and to all my virtual writing companions at GeekMom.com.

The early development of this story goes back to my idea for a feature-length screenplay. Thank you Rick Perez, Pat Anderson, and the Bloomington Playwrights Project for producing a staged reading of *Green Tara*. Before I had developed the novelist's craft of narrative voice, a number of actors, including Meryl Krieger, Jim Hetmer, Cat Richards, brought my story to life. This staged reading was made possible by an Indiana Arts Commission Individual Artist Grant.

Finally, I thank my editors. Sara Grant read the first 50 pages of an early draft at a SCBWI workshop, and invited me to consider rewriting the novel in first person. She thought readers would connect more strongly with the characters, and she was right. Members of the Bloomington Children's Authors group, Elsa Marston, Keiko Kasza, Marilyn Anderson, and Sherry Hudson, gave the manuscript a careful reading and helped focus and strengthen the story. Jennifer Deam, who has been a champion of my stories from my earliest fiction efforts, gave the novel you are reading its final polish.

⊕

Author

K.H. Brower, multi-media storyteller and educator, lives in Bloomington, Indiana. Her home is full of two precocious children, both more gorgeous, strong, and intelligent than she; five warm-blooded pets who shed unmanageable amounts of fur; new and old friends, as often as she can have them over; and a husband, who keeps everyone happy with his delightful whistle and joyful step. She loves to walk on the beach, grow flowers and vegetables, and ride her bicycle.

Feel free to contact her at www.khbrower.com.

Cover Artist

Rea Kersey, illustrator, cartographer, and multi-media developer, lives in Bloomington, Indiana, with her husband, Bill, and sons, Will and Joey. She loves to garden, cook, and create interesting spaces inside and outside her home. When she chuckles, chortles, or throws her head back and laughs, everyone around her joins in.

Sneak Peek of the next book in the series:
Mission to Blue Grannus

The Accident

It's rare when a teenager volunteers to do chores, but I did. I felt trapped in the family space ship and I had ever since we'd left planetary orbit, so I was eager to do anything outside, even clean up. I really did want to sweep out the ion jets.

It meant I got to go all the way outside! Into deep space where all that exists is the cosmic wind.

The problem was chronic. Our ship kept losing power and it had from the beginning of our voyage. The further we traveled, the worse it got. So here we were, stalled out more than we moved, and we still had a long way to go.

My Uncle Leo, the inventor of our trans-light space ship, was systematically testing every possible cause, no matter how far-fetched. He thought we might have picked up trace amounts of organic material, and even a small amount could clog a vent and stall an engine. That's how I can explain my day's chore, to sweep away any planetary stuff that might still be clinging to the ion jets.

"Gordy." Uncle Leo's deep voice invaded my headset, "Report."

"I'm secured and ready. On my way." And I was because, no matter how low the probability I could solve our trans-light velocity failures by sweeping, I wanted to be outside. So there, on the dark side of the hatch, suited up and tethered, I stepped onto the ship's hull.

My gravity boots gave me a sure-footed grip, as I stepped around the spherical, clear bubble that made our family space ship the most distinctive in the galaxy. I made my way along the edge of the wide bubble, which spanned the topside of our ship. The bubble was flanked by two similar, but different, scramjets that Uncle Leo had already customized. On our last planetary stop, he and Aunt Mo harnessed the scramjets to a unifying bubble structure that housed a living biosphere. Below deck our family ship held the living soil of interconnected roots that we'd harvested from the planet Green Tara. Topside, leaves worked their photosynthetic magic, and the plant life gave us a natural source of oxygen. I named our family space ship *The Tree House* because we slept in hammocks hung from living trees. Through the transparent bubble I could see inside our living quarters into the family great room, the galley where we ate, and the hammocks where I'd spent most of the last two years gazing endlessly at the spectacular star view. If you have to fly a long-distance voyage across the galaxy, this was the place to live.

At that moment the central living space was empty of crew because while I was outside they were monitoring my activity from the command and navigation controls inside the scramjets. My cat Spooky ran free, jumping aloft from branch to branch and chasing me from just underneath the transparent dome, as I crossed to the other side of the ship to check for debris. I planned to start on the engine vent furthest from the hatch and then work my way back.

I'm an explorer, and I look forward to the unknown. But stranded out here between worlds, I was bored. There was nothing I could put my hands on, nothing new to experience. Our voyage had dragged on far too long. We were so far from the Tara System, that even though I knew the general direction, I couldn't pick it out by eye. Our destination, the Prime System, wasn't visible either. I stood alone scanning the endless spectacular star scape. I'd seen enough to last a lifetime.

"Gordy?" Uncle Leo spoke through the com line, "Status update."

"I'm in position now." I was under the starboard jets on my cousin Virginia's scramjet, the *Blast*. I turned my head toward the first vent so Uncle Leo and the others could see my camera view.

I opened the vent with a wrench and brushed the flaps, taking care to wipe around the opening, too.

"Do you see any debris?" Uncle Leo asked. I imagined strands of debris springing out of his wiry gray hair. That's the only source of organic debris I could think of out here in deep space.

"No debris," I said. I felt the electrostatic charge of my visor as the macro lens on the camera switched on. I knew Uncle Leo was documenting each vent for any possible interference, even something smaller than my eyes could detect, especially something sticky that didn't blow out the jets.

"No debris?" Virginia echoed my words over the com line. Of course she'd been listening in while I was outside. Even though she never volunteered for chores that didn't involve flying, she always wanted to know what was going on. "I thought you might find some insect goo!" Virginia snorted. She was talking about the first time we entered a viable atmosphere.

"No insect goo," I laughed, too, remembering the juicy wildlife we encountered. Airborne insects clogged the engines then and we almost crashed. We would have, but my cousin is an amazing pilot.

One-step-at-a-time, I leaned toward each of the vents with my wrench and brush, tethered to our ship so I wouldn't float away and leashed to the power source that provided light for my eyes and warmth for my skin.

What I missed the most about our time on a planetary surface were the sunrises and sunsets, the change from night to day and back again, and the way that felt on my skin. Who knew what absolute freedom came from living on a planet, where solar power was free and available for hours at a stretch? Outside the hull of our ship the star view was amazing, but I was encased in a space suit and carried my light on my helmet, so I couldn't feel the texture of anything. I missed the riot of sensations we encountered on our trek through the wilderness, where every step brought something new: scratchy, soft, cool, wet, warm, bright. Out here I found only absolutes. Absolute cold and absolute dark with distant pinpoints of light.

I continued along the engine struts and crossed over to Uncle Leo's *String Machine*, the scramjet with trans-light capabilities. The two-seater, not much bigger than Virginia's *Blast*, worked perfectly when Uncle Leo

I bounced off the bubble surface and rolled the other way. Deep space was so dark and empty. My eyes adjusted and I could see the amazing star view again, but it wasn't enough. I wanted planetary life, with the freedom to roam rocky creek beds and sandy beaches and steep mountain trails. I craved fresh air – the kind filled with a wild mix of odors, sweet and sour, harsh, bold, intoxicating!

At the end of my leash, my suit tugged me back toward *The Tree House*.

Through the tree canopy, I saw Virginia shout something. I'm not a lip reader, but I recognized my name. I put my gloved hand, the one that was still working, on the clear bubble and struggled to get my gravity boots back under me on a framing strut.

"Gordy?!" Uncle Leo shouted again through the com line into my helmet. I knew he was concerned, but the volume shot through my head making it hurt more than my shoulder.

I grunted, hoping he'd turn his volume down.

"I'm coming to get you," he said. "Hang on."

In my head I said I was fine and could make it back inside without any help. But nothing came out of my mouth.

I crawled to the hatch and it sprung open.

To be continued …

⊕